THE LORDS OF INVENTION

Written and digitally painted by Trenor Rapkins

Lettering by Blambot

Copyright 2021

LADIES AND GENTLEMAN.

THANK YOU ALL FOR COMING OUT TONIGHT.

AND NOW FOR THE MOMENT THAT WE HAVE ALL BEEN WAITING FOR . . .

CHOK

MANY OF YOU KNOW HIM AS THE INVENTOR OF THE TELECOMMUNICATOR AND THE AMAZING AUTOMENTIUM MACHINE - - -

BUT AFTER TONIGHT HE WILL BE KNOWN FOR MANY OTHER ACCOMPLISHMENTS AS WELL.

PLEASE NOW WELCOME ONE OF THE GREATEST MINDS OF OUR TIME . . .

AUGUSTUS SCOTT!
CLAP
CLAP
CLAP
CLAP
CLAP
CLAP
CLAP
CLAP
CLAP
CLAP
CLAP
CLAP
CLAP
CLAP
CLAP

CLAP
CLAP
CLAP
CLAP
CLAP
CLAP

THANK YOU.
THANK YOU VERY MUCH.

GOOD EVENING LADIES AND GENTEMEN. THANK YOU FOR YOUR ATTENDANCE. I HAVE BEEN LOOKING FORWARD TO THIS MOMENT FOR A LONG TIME.
TONIGHT I WILL REVEAL FOR THE VERY FIRST TIME TWELVE NEW INVENTIONS.

BEFORE WE BEGIN I WOULD LIKE TO TELL YOU A LITTLE ABOUT MYSELF.
I WAS BORN AND RAISED IN NEW HAMPSHIRE.
MY FATHER WAS A LAWYER AND MY MOTHER WAS A TEACHER.
UNFORTUNATELY FOR HER, ONE OF HER STUDENTS WAS ME.

HAHA
HAHA
HAHAHA

IN SCHOOL I WAS REPRIMANDED CONSTANTLY FOR THE TRANSGRESSION OF DAYDREAMING.
ALTHOUGH, I DID EVENTUALLY APPLY MYSELF AS I BECAME OLDER, WHICH MADE IT POSSIBLE TO ATTEND DARTMOUTH COLLEGE.

HOWEVER, I NEVER DID COMPLETE MY CONVENTIONAL STUDIES. THIS IS BECAUSE I HAD MORE PRESSING MATTERS TO ATTEND TO. AMONG WHICH IS WHAT HAS COME TO BE REFERRED TO AS THE AUTOMENTIUM MACHINE.
MY SUCCESS IN THAT ENDEAVOR, AND OTHERS, HAS ALLOWED ME TO WORK INDEPENDENTLY.

EIGHT YEARS AGO I RELOCATED HERE TO NEW YORK, WHERE I NOW HAVE A STUDIO A LITTLE MORE THAN THIRTY MILES FROM THIS LOCATION, AND WHERE MOST OF THE INVENTIONS THAT WILL BE DISPLAYED TONIGHT WERE CONCEIVED.
AND NOW I SHALL REVEAL THE FIRST OF THESE CREATIONS: A FULLY FUNCTIONAL AUTOMATON.
A MACHINE THAT WILL CARRY OUT OUR MOST DANGEROUS AND TIRESOME TASKS.
LADIES AND GENTLEMEN, I PRESENT TO YOU . . .

ADAM!

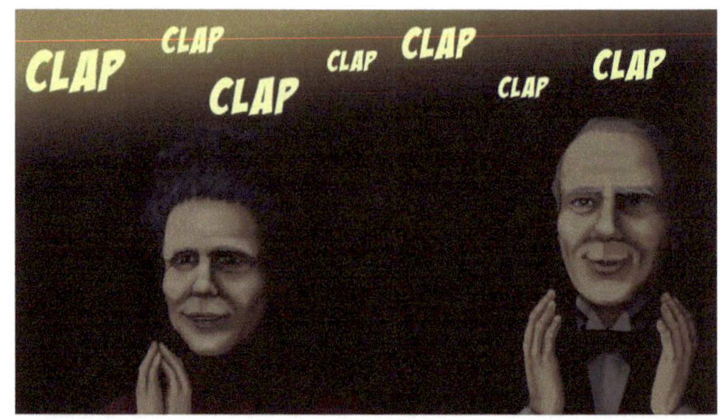

CLAP
CLAP
CLAP
CLAP
CLAP
CLAP
CLAP

ADAM!
COME HERE!

HISSSSHHHHHHHH

CHUG
CHUG
CHUG
CREEEK

CLAP
CLAP
CLAP
CLAP
CLAP
CLAP
CLAP
CLAP
CLAP
CLAP

ALL RIGHT.
NOW SHOW US WHAT YOU CAN DO.

KSHHHHH
KSHHHHH
KSHHHHH
CLAP
CLAP
CLAP
CLAP
CLAP

LADIES AND GENTLEMEN, I HAVE SOMETHING TO REVEAL TO YOU.
ADAM DOES NOT HAVE HIS OWN BRAIN. HE IS ACTUALLY BEING OPERATED REMOTELY.
IF YOU LOOK TO YOUR LEFT YOU WILL SEE MY ASSISTANT OPERATING MACHINERY THAT CONTROLS THE ELECTRICAL SIGNALS THAT ARE TRAVELING THROUGH THE AIR AND TELLING ADAM WHAT TO DO.

CLAP
CLAP
CLAP
CLAP
CLAP
HELLO BENNY!

THANK YOU ADAM. GOOD BYE.
CLAP
CLAP
CLAP
CLAP

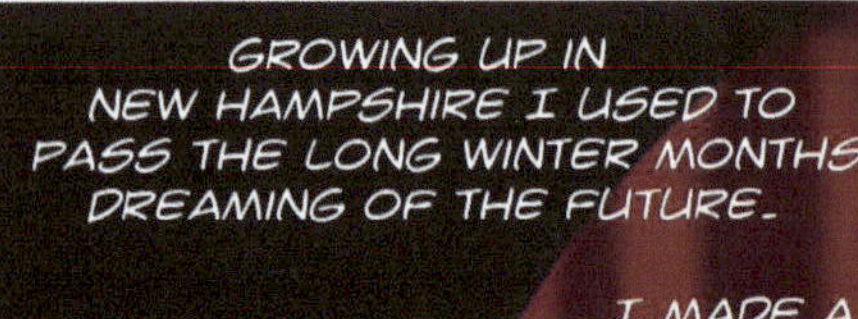

GROWING UP IN NEW HAMPSHIRE I USED TO PASS THE LONG WINTER MONTHS DREAMING OF THE FUTURE.
I MADE A VOW THAT I WOULD ONE DAY UNDERSTAND THE LAWS OF NATURE.
SO BEGAN MY INTEREST IN THE STUDY OF ELECTRO-MAGNETICS.
THENCEFORTH I WORKED ON DEVISING A CONTRAPTION THAT COULD AMPLIFY MAGNETIC FORCE.
I REFER TO THIS CONCEPTION AS . . .

THE ELECTROMAGTRONICON.

WHEN MY ASSISTANT ACTIVATES THE SWITCH YOU WILL SEE THE MAGIC OF SCIENCE TAKE PLACE.

AND THREE . . .
TWO . . .
ONE . . .
ACTIVATE!

CLICK

LADIES AND GENTLEMEN, I PRESENT TO YOU . . .
BZZZZZZZZZZZZZZ

LEVITATION!

CLAP
CLAP
CLAP
CLAP
CLAP
CLAP
CLAP

THIS IS NOT A MAGIC TRICK!
THIS IS NOT AN ILLUSION!
THIS IS SCIENCE!

CLICK

BZZZZZZZZZZZZZ

ANOTHER CHILDHOOD DREAM OF MINE IS THE SAME AS MANY OTHERS I SUPPOSE.
I AM TALKING ABOUT THE DREAM OF FLIGHT.
TONIGHT THAT DREAM WILL BE BECOME REALITY.
USING A NEWLY DISCOVERED LIGHT-THAN-AIR GAS CALLED HELIUM, I HAVE CREATED A CONTRAPTION THAT CAN LIFT MAN INTO THE SKY.
BEHOLD!

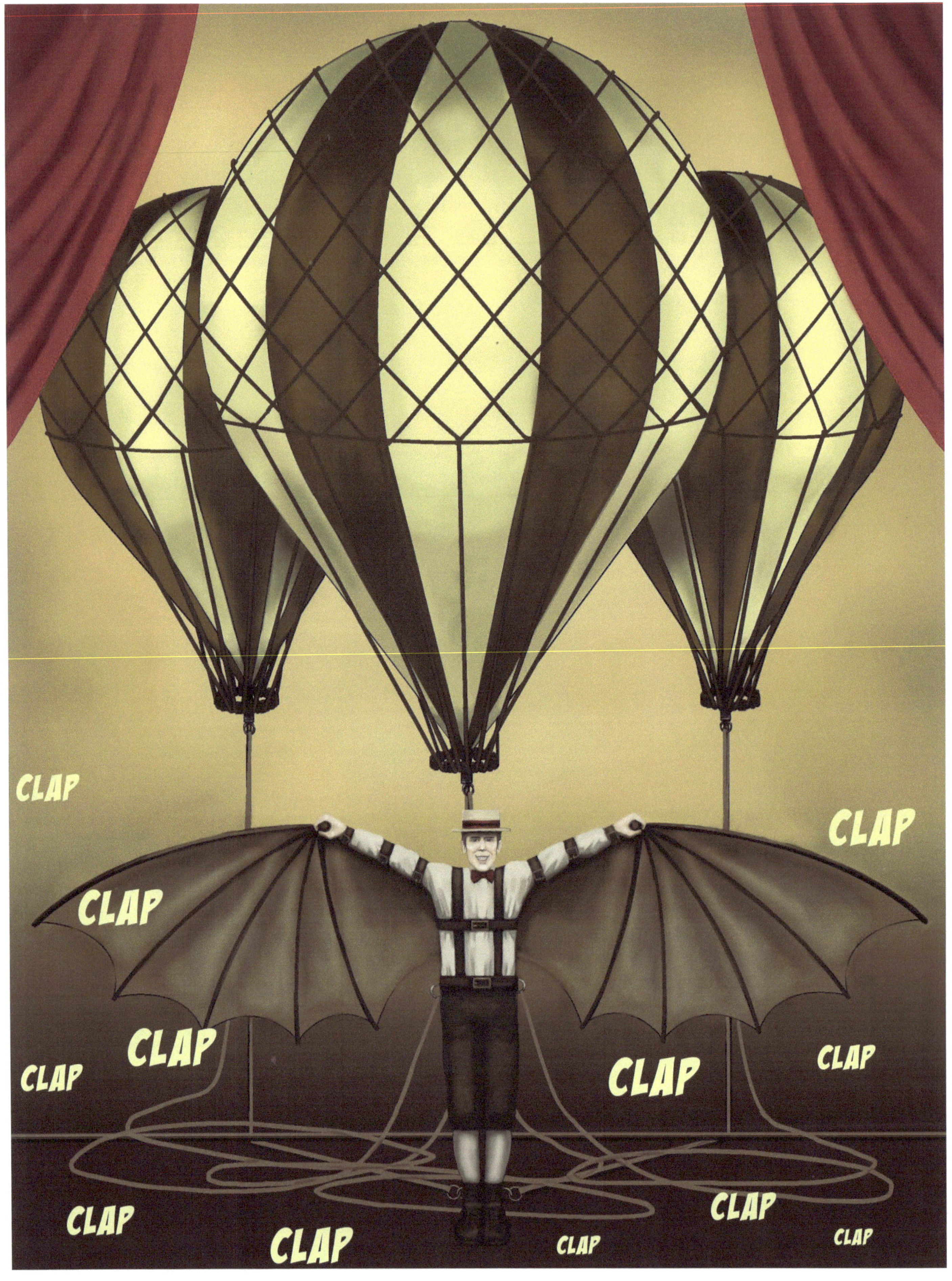
CLAP
CLAP
CLAP
CLAP
CLAP
CLAP
CLAP
CLAP
CLAP
CLAP
CLAP
CLAP

LADIES AND GENTLEMEN!
I GIVE YOU . . .
HUMAN FLIGHT!

CLAP
CLAP
CLAP
CLAP
CLAP
CLAP
CLAP

CLAP
CLAP
CLAP
CLAP
CLAP
CLAP
CLAP
WE WILL ALL FLY! LIMITLESS AND FREE!

CLAP
CLAP
CLAP
CLAP
CLAP
CLAP

CLAP
CLAP
CLAP
CLAP
CLAP

CLAP
CLAP
CLAP

GET UP!

I SAID
GET UP!

HEY!

AAAAAA!

CREEEEEEEEK

CLICK

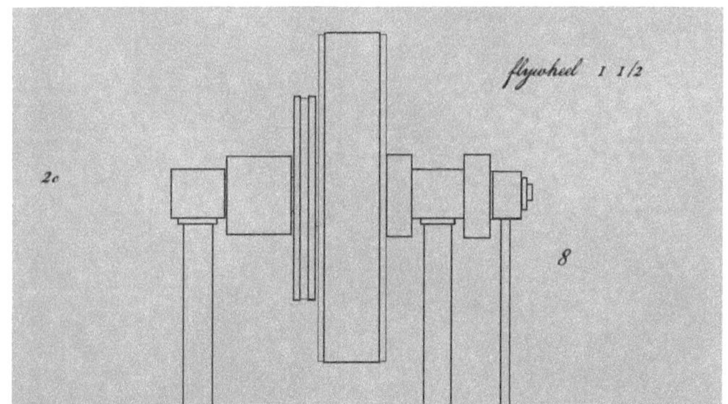

flywheel 1 1/2
2c
8

DAMN_

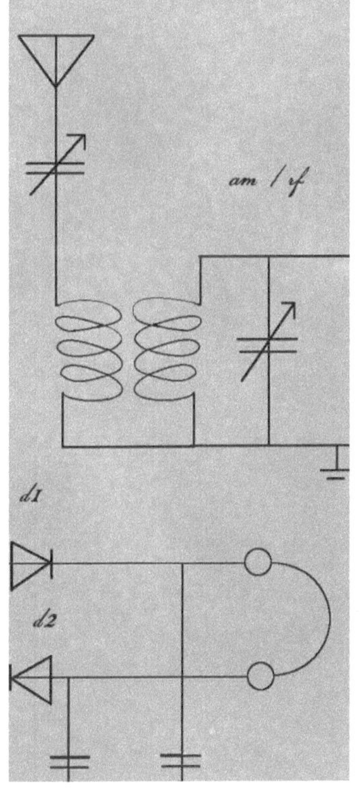

am / if
d1
d2

DAMN IT ALL_

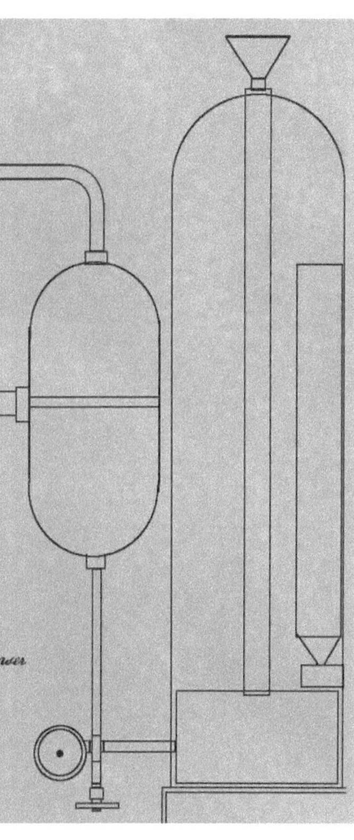

DAMN IT ALL!
KSSHHHHHHHH
KaChoOSh

The
Lords of
Invention

BRINNNNNNNNG

NOK
NOK
ARE YOU DECENT?
YES.

GOOD MORNING.

WE HAVE SOMETHING FOR YOU.
BREAKFAST IN BED? WHAT IS THE OCCASION?

YOU LEAVE FOR EUROPE TODAY. HAVE YOU FORGOTTEN?

WHAT IS EUROPE?

EUROPE IS VERY FAR AWAY.
THAT IS WHY I WILL BE GONE FOR SO LONG.

WHY DO YOU HAVE TO GO TO EUROPE?

BECAUSE HE HAS TO SHOW HIS INVENTIONS TO PEOPLE WHO HAVEN'T SEEN THEM YET.

NOW EMILY, YOU ARE GOING TO BE GOOD WHILE I'M GONE, RIGHT?

YEEES.

IF YOU ARE GOOD THEN MAYBE I WILL BRING YOU A PRESENT. YOU WANT A PRESENT RIGHT?

I WANT A PUPPY!

MAYBE WHEN YOU ARE OLD ENOUGH TO TAKE CARE OF A DOG BY YOURSELF THEN MAYBE YOU CAN HAVE A PUPPY. BUT YOU ARE NOT OLD ENOUGH YET.

WHEN I AM SEVEN YEARS OLD, THEN CAN I HAVE A PUPPY?

HA HA HA!

NOK NOK
WAS THAT A KNOCK?

IT'S PROBABLY BENNY.

I'LL GET IT!

HELLO EMILY.

GOOD MORNING BENNY.

GOOD MORNING.
I HOPE THAT I AM NOT TOO EARLY.

AUGUSTUS IS STILL WAKING UP, BUT DO COME IN.
WOULD YOU LIKE SOME COFFEE OR SOMETHING TO EAT?

I ALREADY ATE BUT SOME COFFEE WOULD BE APPRECIATED.

LATER THAT MORNING.

GOOD MORNING.

GOOD MORNING GENTLEMEN.
ARE YOU READY FOR A GRAND ADVENTURE?

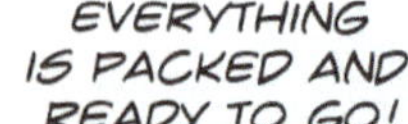

EVERYTHING IS PACKED AND READY TO GO!

VERY WELL THEN. ALLOW ME A MOMENT.
I WILL BE WITH YOU SHORTLY.

ABSOLUTELY!

WELL MY DEARS, IT IS TIME TO GO.

REMEMBER TO BE GOOD WHILE I AM AWAY.

GOOD BYE.

REMEMBER TO WRITE AT LEAST ONE LETTER.
I WILL WRITE MORE THAN ONE LETTER.
I PROMISE.

ALL RIGHT!
IT IS TIME TO DEPART!

GOOD BYE MY LOVES.

FAREWELL.

GOOD BYE!
GOOD BYE EMILY AND MISSES SCOTT!

GOOD BYE AND GOOD LUCK!

AND HERE WE GO!

WHAT'S WRONG?
DID YOU FORGET SOMETHING?

NO.
I JUST ALREADY MISS THEM.

ALL RIGHT!
THAT'S ALL FOR TODAY!
GO HOME!

EVENING TELEGRAM HERE!

THANK YOU SIR.

PEANUTS
5¢ per package

Evening Telegram
FINAL
AUGUSTUS ASTOUNDS AGAIN
EXTRA

CHUG
CHUG
CHUG

KSHHHHHHHHH

I HAVE BEEN A FANCIER OF THE MANHATTAN GIANTS FROM THE VERY BEGINNING, BACK WHEN THEY STILL REFERRED TO THEMSELVES AS THE GOTHAMS.

UNLIKE MANY OTHERS, I STAYED LOYAL EVEN DURING THE UNFORTUNATE TIMES.

AND WHEN YOU STAY LOYAL TO YOUR TEAM DURING THE UNFORUTNATE TIMES IT MAKES THE FORTUNATE TIMES EVEN BETTER.

EXCUSE US PLEASE, BUT ARE YOU AUGUSTUS SCOTT?
I AM.

WE ARE FANCIERS OF YOUR WORK. ESPECIALLY THE FLYING HELIUM BALLOON.
THANK YOU VERY MUCH.

WE WERE WONDERING WHAT NEW INVEVTIONS YOU HAVE IN STORE.

WELL, IT IS A MATTER OF UTMOST SECRECY, BUT I SUPPOSE THAT I CAN CONFIDE IN YOU, PROVIDED THAT THE BOTH OF YOU PROMISE TO UPHOLD THE CONFIDENTIALITY THAT IS REQUIRED.

WE PROMISE.

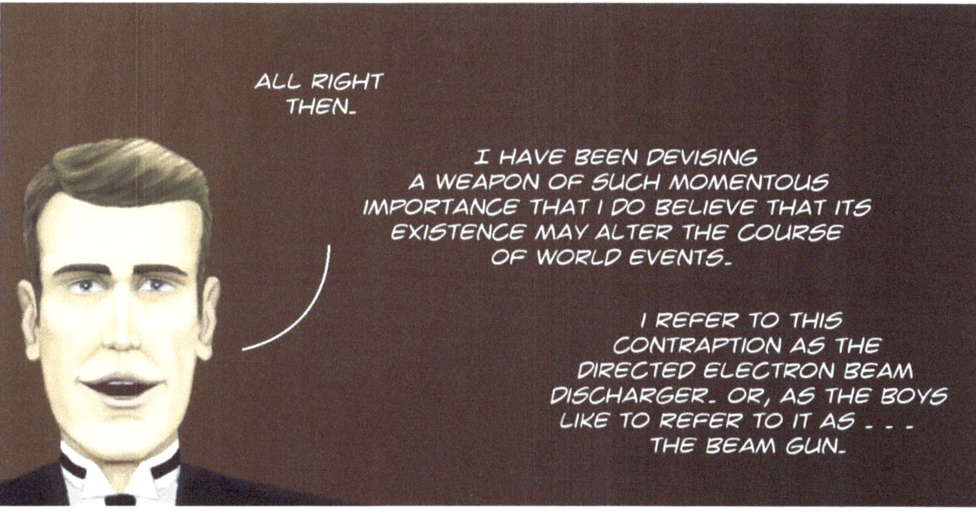

ALL RIGHT THEN.
I HAVE BEEN DEVISING A WEAPON OF SUCH MOMENTOUS IMPORTANCE THAT I DO BELIEVE THAT ITS EXISTENCE MAY ALTER THE COURSE OF WORLD EVENTS.
I REFER TO THIS CONTRAPTION AS THE DIRECTED ELECTRON BEAM DISCHARGER. OR, AS THE BOYS LIKE TO REFER TO IT AS . . . THE BEAM GUN.

SOUNDS BRILLIANT.

NOW REMEMBER. YOU LADIES BOTH PROMISED NOT TO REVEAL THIS INFORMATION TO ANYONE.
NOT EVEN A SINGLE SOUL.

YES, WE BOTH PROMISE.

VERY WELL THEN.
CHEERS.

IT WAS NICE TO MEET YOU. GOOD DAY TO YOU.
AND TO YOU AS WELL. GOODBYE.

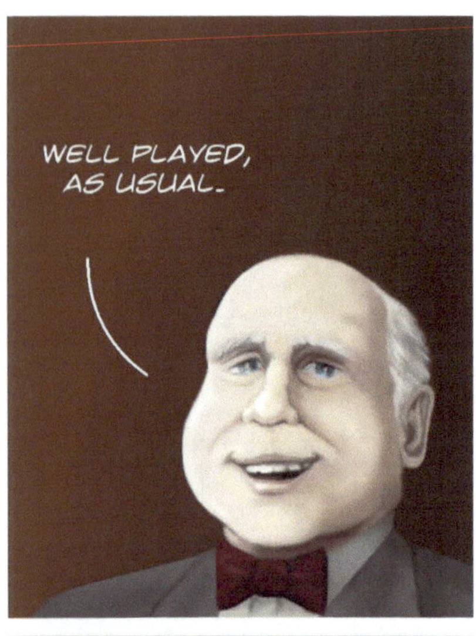

WELL PLAYED, AS USUAL.

IT MUST NICE TO ENJOY THE ADMIRATION OF SUCH BEAUTIFUL WOMAN AS THAT.

OH WERE THEY BEAUTIFUL?
THERE IS ONLY ONE BEAUTIFUL WOMAN IN MY LIFE.
I DO NOT EVEN NOTICE THE OTHERS.

AND NOW THAT WE ARE FINISHED HERE, SHALL WE ADJOURN TO THE DECK TO ENJOY SOME FINE CIGARS?

HEAR HEAR.

AUGH!

HEY PICKETT!
IF YOU CAN'T DO THIS JOB THEN LET ME KNOW AND I WILL GET SOMEONE WHO CAN!

CHUK

MAMA.

MAMA WAKE UP.

EMILY? WHAT IS IT?
I'M SCARED.

WHAT IS THERE TO BE SCARED OF?

THERE IS SOMEONE IN PAPA'S OFFICE.

OH EMILY.
THE WINDOW WAS PROBABLY LEFT OPEN.
IT'S JUST THE WIND.

NO, IT'S SOMEONE.

ALL RIGHT,
I WILL GO LOOK.
YOU WAIT HERE.

CHOK

LONDON, ENGLAND

AND HERE WE ARE.

WELL GEORGE, I HAVE TO SAY THAT YOU HAVE GOT QUITE A MACHINE HERE, BUT I STILL SAY THAT THE COMBUSTION ENGINE DOES NOT HAVE THE ADVANTAGES THAT MY ELECTRIC CARRIAGE HAS.
MARK MY WORDS: THE FUTRE BELONGS TO ELECTRIC.

HAHA. TIME WILL TELL. TIME WILL TELL.

I AM STARVING. DOES THIS HOTEL HAVE A RESTAURANT?
YES IT DOES. LET'S GET SOME LUNCH AND PLAN THE FUTURE.

MISTER SCOTT. MAY I SPEAK WITH YOU?

CERTAINLY, ALTHOUGH I WAS JUST ON THE WAY TO GET SOME LUNCH WITH MY NEW FRIEND HERE. CAN IT WAIT UNTIL LATER?

I AM VERY SORRY, BUT I AM AFRAID THAT IT IS VERY NECESSARY THAT I TALK TO YOU IN PRIVATE IMMEDIATELY.

ALL RIGHT THEN.
EXCUSE ME GEORGE.
QUITE ALL RIGHT.
I WILL GET STARTED
WITHOUT YOU.

PLEASE
TAKE A
SEAT.
SO WHAT
IS THIS ALL
ABOUT?

WE RECEIVED
A VERY IMPORTANT
MESSAGE FOR YOU WHILE
YOU WERE OUT.
I AM AFRAID THAT
I HAVE VERY UNFORTUNATE
NEWS TO REPORT.

WHAT IS THE
MATTER?

THERE WAS
A FIRE AT YOUR
HOUSE IN NEW YORK.
A VERY BAD FIRE.
I AM SORRY
TO HAVE TO INFORM
YOU THAT YOUR WIFE
AND DAUGHTER WERE
SERIOUSLY HARMED.

WHAT DO YOU
MEAN, HARMED?

I'M VERY SORRY,
BUT THE WORD THAT WE
RECEIVED IS THAT THEY
DID NOT SURVIVE.

I AM SO SORRY.
IF THERE IS ANYTHING I CAN DO, PLEASE LET ME KNOW.

HOW DID THE FIRE HAPPEN?

I DO NOT KNOW. WE WERE NOT TOLD.

CAN YOU PLEASE GIVE ME A MOMENT IN HERE BY MYSELF?

OF COURSE. TAKE AS MUCH TIME AS YOU NEED.

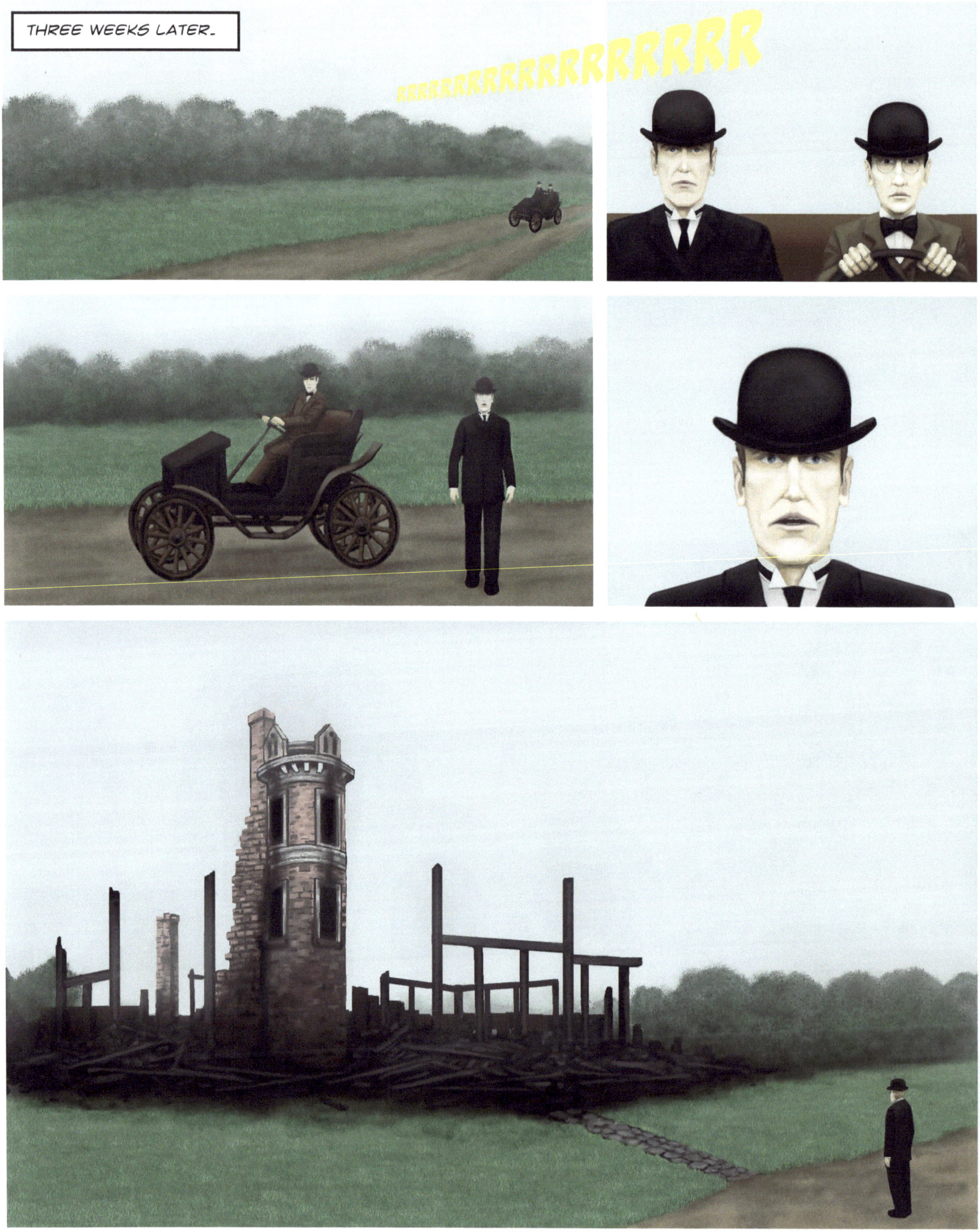

THREE WEEKS LATER.

RRRRRRRRRRRRRRRR

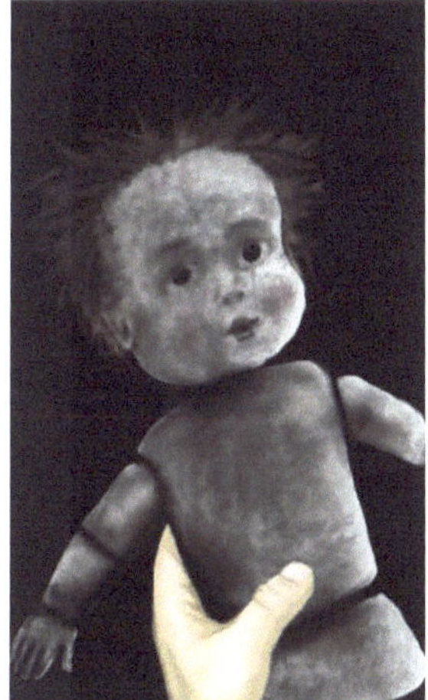

BRINNNNNNNING

HELLO.

YES, HELLO
MISTER SCOTT.

THIS IS DETECTIVE
O'MALLEY.

I AM THE ONE
WHO IS INVESTIGATING
THE INCIDENT THAT OCCURRED
AT YOUR RESIDENCE.

I REALIZE THAT THINGS MUST BE VERY DIFFICULT FOR YOU RIGHT NOW, HOWEVER, YOU SHOULD KNOW ABOUT A SIGNIFICANT DEVELOPMENT THAT HAS ARISEN.
THE FIRE DEPARTMENT HAS CONFIRMED THAT THE CAUSE OF THE FIRE IS SUSPICIOUS. ALSO, WHEN YOUR WIFE'S REMAINS WERE FOUND IT APPEARED THAT HER HANDS HAD BEEN BOUND BEHIND HER BACK.
NOW I NEED TO KNOW IF YOU HAVE ANY ENEMIES THAT I NEED TO KNOW ABOUT.

ENEMIES? NO, I MEAN . . . I DON'T KNOW.
ARE YOU TELLING ME THAT MY WIFE AND DAUGHTER WERE MURDERED?

THE EVIDENCE SEEMS TO BE INDICATING THAT. YES.

I HAVE NO IDEA WHO WOULD DO SUCH A THING.

IF YOU CAN'T THINK OF ANY SUSPECTS NOW I UNDERSTAND. I ONLY REQUEST THAT YOU GIVE THE MATTER FURTHER THOUGHT.
THIS COULD ALSO JUST BE A RANDOM BURGLARY AND YOU MAY NOT KNOW THE INTRUDER.
HOWEVER, I DO NEED YOU TO CONTACT ME IF ANYONE COMES TO MIND.

YES, OF COURSE.

I WILL BE SURE TO CONTACT YOU IF WE DISCOVER ANYTHING ELSE.
BYE FOR NOW.

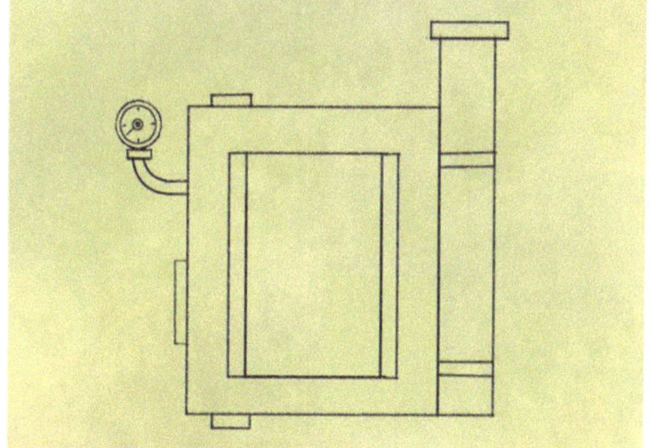

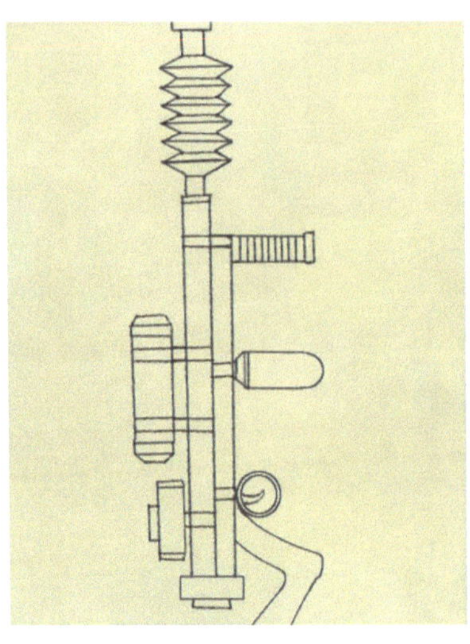

POISON
LAUDANUM
UPPER CASE SMALL CAPS & SPECIALS
$10

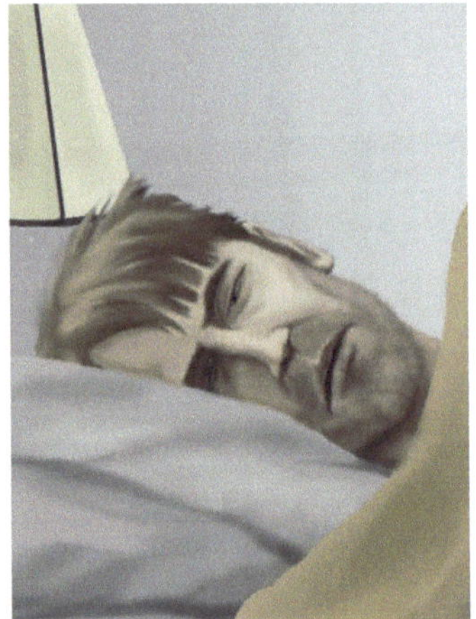

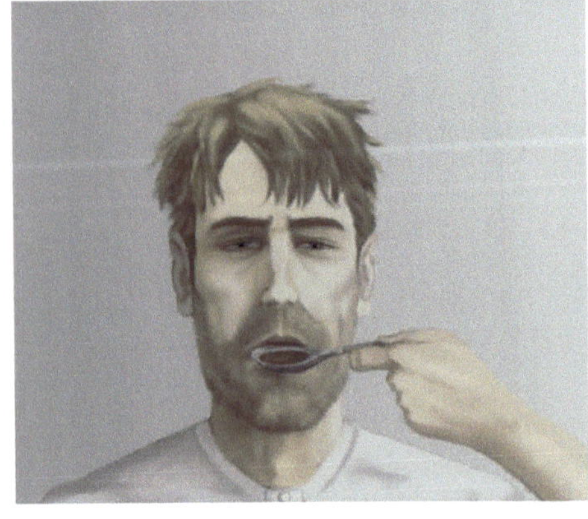

OF COURSE.

OF COURSE.

OF COURSE!

BRINNNNG

YES?
GOOD MORNING MISTER SCOTT.
THERE IS A MISTER HIRSCHFELD HERE TO SEE YOU.

- - - YES, ALL RIGHT.
SEND HIM UP.

NOK
NOK

ENTER.

HELLO BENNY.

GOOD MORNING.

ARE YOU AWARE THAT LAUDANUM IS POISONOUS?

WELL, YOU REALLY SHOULD AT LEAST LET ROOM SERVICE IN HERE ONCE IN A WHILE TO TIDY THINGS UP.

I AM ALWAYS IN HERE.
I WOULD JUST BE IN THEIR WAY.

IN THAT CASE MAYBE YOU NEED TO GET OUT MORE.

AND GO WHERE?

HOW ABOUT BACK TO THE LABORATORY? HOW ABOUT BACK TO WORK? IT WOULD BE A GREAT WAY TO GET YOUR MIND OFF OF THINGS.

I APPRECIATE YOUR OPTIMISM MY BULLY OLD CHUM, BUT I AM ALL OUT OF IDEAS.

I FIND THAT DIFFICULT TO BELIEVE.

YOU ARE A GOOD MAN BENNY, AND I APPRECIATE WHAT YOU ARE TRYING TO DO, BUT YOU HAVE WASTED YOUR TIME BY COMING HERE.

WHAT ARE YOU GOING TO DO? WASTE AWAY IN A DARK HOTEL ROOM FOR THE REST OF YOUR LIFE, GETTING NUMB AND DWELLING IN THE PAST? YOU ARE MAKING IT WORSE BY NOT MOVING FORWARD.

WHERE THE HEART GOES SO DOES THE SPIRIT, AND SO GOES THE MIND. MY HEART IS BROKEN BENNY. EVERYTHING ELSE IS TRIVIAL BY COMPARISON.

I THANK YOU FOR STOPPING BY, BUT I REALLY HAVE NO DESIRE TO GO ON AS IF NOTHING HAS HAPPENED. I HAVE NO DESIRE TO START ALL OVER AGAIN. AT LEAST NOT YET.

NOW, IF THERE IS NOTHING MORE, I MUST ASK YOU TO PARDON ME.

AS YOU WISH.

I HOPE TO WORK WITH YOU AGAIN ONE DAY.
GOOD BYE FOR NOW.

GOOD BYE BENNY.

KA CHUNK

CREEEEEK

CLICK

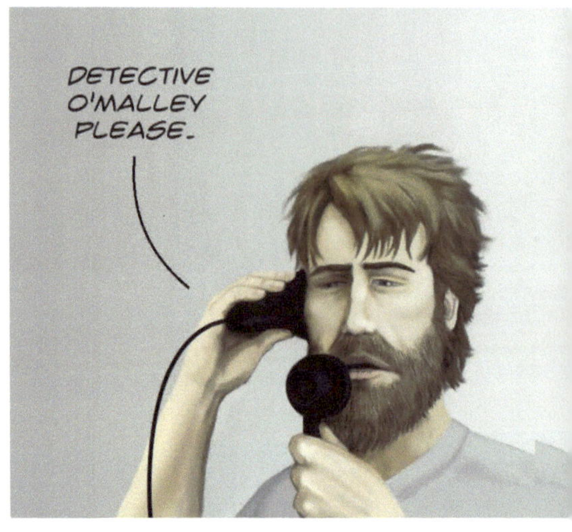

DETECTIVE O'MALLEY PLEASE.

THIS IS DETECTIVE O'MALLEY.

HELLO DETECTIVE. THIS IS AUGUSTUS SCOTT.

YES MISTER SCOTT. WHAT CAN I DO FOR YOU?

I WAS WONDERING HOW MY CASE WAS GOING AND IF YOU HAD ANY NEW INFORMATION FOR ME?

I AM SORRY TO REPORT THAT I DO NOT HAVE ANY NEW INFORMATION FOR YOU AT THIS TIME.
HOWEVER, THE INVESTIGATION IS STILL UNDERWAY.

I SEE . . . I THANK YOU ANYWAY.

AS SOON AS
ANY DEVELOPMENTS
ARISE YOU CAN DEPEND
ON ME TO CONTACT
YOU.

YES,
I UNDERSTAND.
THANK YOU AGAIN.
GOOD BYE.

GOOD BYE.

NOK
NOK

ENTER.

YOU MUST
BE MISTER
PICKETT.

I AM.

YOU WILL
NEED TO BE
QUICK. I HAVE
TO LEAVE
SOON.

YES SIR.
I HAVE, ON THESE SHEETS OF PAPER, THE DESIGNS FOR A GROUND-BREAKING INVENTION OF THE FUTURE.

HERE IT IS.

WHAT IS THIS?

THAT IS THE ELECTRO-GUN.

WHAT DOES IT DO?

IN ORDER TO UNDERSTAND WHAT IT DOES YOU MUST FIRST UNDERSTAND THAT EVERYTHING IN THE FUTURE WILL BE POWERED BY ELECTRICITY, INCLUDING THE MILITARY.
THE ELECTRO-GUN HAS THE ABILITY TO OVERLOAD ELECTRIC SYSTEMS, THEREBY DISABLING THEM.
HOWEVER, THIS IS NOT ITS ONLY ABILITY.
THE DEVICE ALSO EMITS A BEAM OF ENERGY OF SUCH POWER THAT IT CAN ELECTROCUTE BIOLOGICAL TARGETS.

BIOLOGICAL TARGETS?

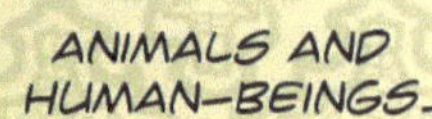

ANIMALS AND HUMAN-BEINGS.
AND, UNLIKE REGULAR WEAPONS, IT IS NEARLY SILENT AND HAS A MUCH LONGER RANGE THAN TRADITIONAL SILENT WEAPONS, AND IS MUCH MORE ACCURATE AS WELL.
WHAT YOU SEE BEFORE YOU IS THE FUTURE OF MODERN-DAY LAW-ENFORCEMENT AND WARFARE.

IN ORDER TO CONSTRUCT A WORKING MODEL I REQUIRE ADDITIONAL FUNDING. IF YOU INVEST IN THIS PROJECT I WILL SEE TO IT THAT YOU WILL NOT REGRET IT.

HMMM . . .

WELL, I DON'T HAVE THE TIME TO GET INTO THIS NOW, HOWEVER I WOULD LIKE TO INVESTIGATE THIS MATTER FURTHER WITH YOU AT A BETTER TIME.
HOW DOES THAT SOUND TO YOU?

THAT SOUNDS GREAT SIR.
THANK YOU.

ALL RIGHT THEN. I WILL SEE YOU LATER.
GOODBYE SIR. THANK YOU FOR YOUR TIME.

JOHNSON'S PHARMACY
15

PARDON ME SIR.

WHAT IS IT?

ARE YOU AUGUSTUS SCOTT?

NO.

GOOD AFTERNOON SIR. WHAT'LL IT BE?

LAUDANUM.

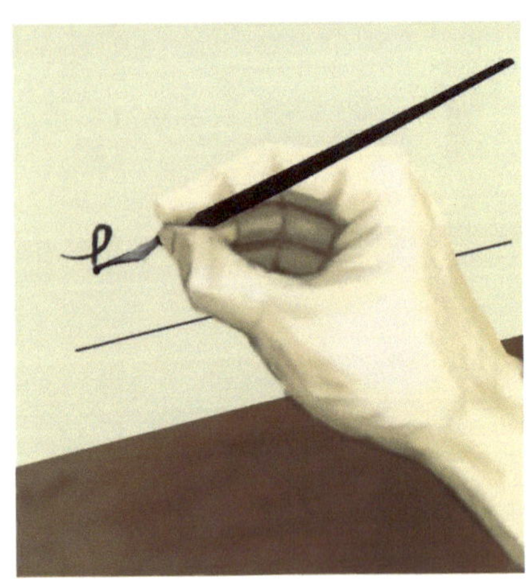

Levi Pickett

THERE IT IS MISTER MONROE.
I DO BELIEVE THAT WE ARE OFFICIAL NOW.

INDEED WE ARE MISTER PICKETT.

INDEED WE ARE.

CLICK

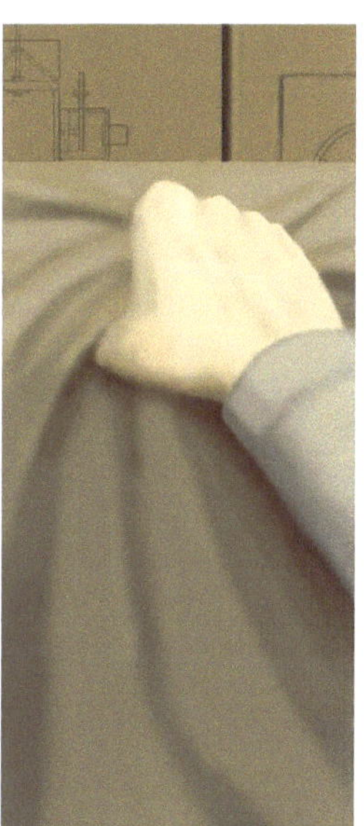

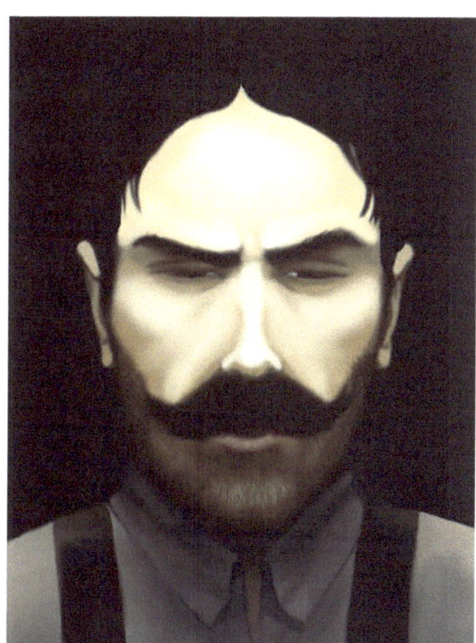

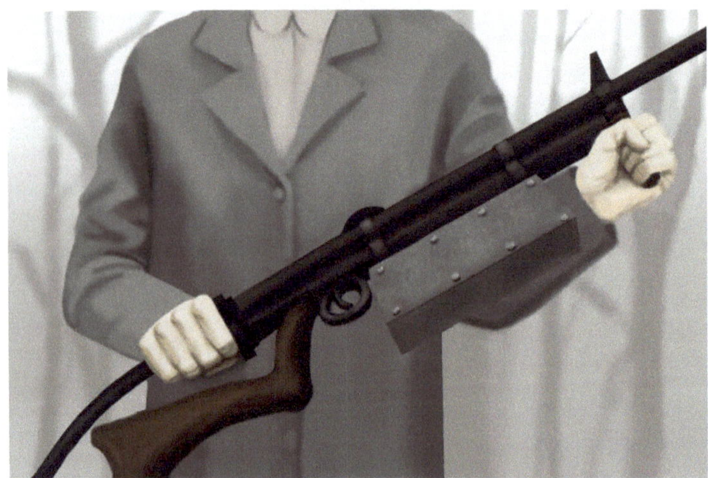

CHUK

SHUK

CLICK

BERBERBERBERBERBERBERBER

CAW
CAW
CAW

BZZZzzzzzzzzz

KRAK
CAAA!

HAHAAA!

PICKETT!
WHY ARE YOU LATE AND WHY ARE YOU DRESSED LIKE THAT?

I MUST INFORM YOU SIR THAT I HAVE AN UPDATE CONCERNING THE STATUS OF MY SITUATION.

OH REALLY, AND WHAT'S THAT?

I QUIT

ZZZZZZZZZZZZZZZZ

KRAK
SCREEEE!

DEAD.

NOT ONLY DOES THE ELECTRO-GUN TERMINATE BIOLOGICAL TARGETS BUT IT DISABLES ELECTRONIC TARGETS AS WELL.

AND IT IS QUIETER AND MORE ACCURATE FROM DISTANCE THAN A REGULAR FIREARM.

VERY IMPRESSIVE.
I DO BELIEVE THAT THE WAR DEPARTMENT WOULD BE VERY MUCH INTERESTED IN YOUR WEAPON.

EXCELLENT!

KELLY'S OLD ALE HOUSE
15

HELLO AUGUSTUS.

BENNY.
HOW DID YOU FIND ME?

THE BELLBOY AT THE HOTEL SAID THAT YOU WOULD MOST LIKELY BE AT ONE OF THE NEARBY DOGGERIES GETTING SOAKED.

AT LEAST YOU'RE GETTING OUT OF THE HOTEL NOW. THAT'S A GOOD SIGN.

SO WHAT IS IT THAT I CAN DO FOR YOU?

I SUPPOSE YOU DO NOT READ THE NEWSPAPER ANYMORE, SO I BROUGHT ONE TO YOU.

YOU'RE RIGHT. WHAT DOES IT SAY?

IT SAYS THAT ANOTHER INVENTOR BEAT YOU TO THE BEAM-GUN.
ALTHOUGH HE IS REFERRING TO IT AS THE ELECTRO-GUN.

SO HE BEAT ME TO IT.
PERHAPS I WILL SEND HIM A LETTER OF CONGRATULATIONS.

STOP DRINKING FOR A MOMENT. YOU DON'T UNDERSTAND.
THE DESIGN IS ALMOST AN EXACT REPLICA OF YOUR OWN.
HE MUST HAVE BEEN ABLE TO SOLVE THE BEAM DISSAPATION PROBLEM.

AND THE INVENTOR EVEN LIVES RIGHT HERE IN NEW YORK.
DO YOU KNOW WHAT THE ODDS OF THIS IS?

SO WHAT ARE YOU SAYING?

I THINK THE MAN WHO IS CLAIMING TO BE THE INVENTOR, THIS . . .
"LEVI PICKETT."

I THINK THIS IS THE MAN WHO BROKE INTO YOUR HOME AND STOLE THE PLANS TO YOUR INVENTION.
MOLLY MUST HAVE CAUGHT HIM IN THE ACT.
IN ORDER TO COVER UP HIS CRIME HE SET FIRE TO THE HOUSE.

ALL RIGHT.
WE HAVE TO GET THE POLICE TO SEARCH HIS PREMISES FOR EVIDENCE.
I WILL CONTACT DETECTIVE O'MALLEY RIGHT AWAY.
WELL DONE BENNY.

WELL DONE.

PERHAPS YOU CAN HELP ME. I AM LOOKING FOR LEVI PICKETT.
DOES HE RESIDE HERE?

I AM THE MAN THAT YOU ARE LOOKING FOR.
HOW MAY I BE OF ASSISTANCE?

IT HAS COME TO MY ATTENTION THAT YOU HAVE RECENTLY INVENTED A SPECIAL TYPE OF ELECTRICAL WEAPON.
IS THAT TRUE?

GOOD AFTERNOON SIR.

YES.
THAT IS CORRECT.

THAT IS QUITE A CONTRAPTION FROM WHAT I HEAR.
MAY I ASK:
WHERE EXACTLY DID YOU GET THE IDEA FOR YOUR INVENTION?

I GOT THE IDEA FROM MOTHER NATURE.
WHY?

WELL, YOU SHOULD KNOW THAT AUGUSTUS SCOTT IS CHALLENGING THAT CLAIM.
I'M SURE YOU KNOW WHO MISTER SCOTT IS.

YES, I AM FAMILIAR WITH THE MAN.
UNFORTUNATELY FOR HIM I BEAT HIM TO IT AND I HAVE THE PATENT TO PROVE IT.

WOULD YOU MIND IF I TOOK A LOOK AT THE PLANS FOR THE INVENTION?

NOT AT ALL.
FOLLOW ME INSIDE.

I APPRECIATE YOUR COOPERATION.

Levi William Pickett
Former residence:
220 Henry Street,
New York
Basement dwelling.
Vacated March 30, 190
rrent residence:
04 Fargo Lane,
rvington, New York
SORRY I'M LATE.

THINGS HAVE BEEN TOO BUSY AROUND HERE LATELY.

I UNDERSTAND.

ALL RIGHT THEN. WE QUESTIONED MISTER PICKETT. HE HANDED OVER THESE DOCUMENTS, WHICH HE SAYS ARE THE PLANS FOR HIS ELECTRO-GUN.
I WANTED YOU TO VIEW THESE FOR YOURSELF AND TELL ME WHAT YOU THINK.

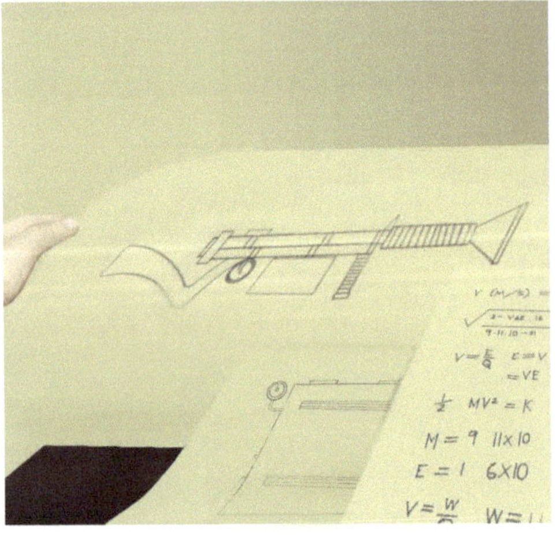

HE OBVIOUSLY JUST REWROTE WHAT I DID.
THIS MEANS NOTHING.

YES. THAT COULD VERY WELL BE THE CASE. HOWEVER, WE ALSO SEARCHED BOTH HIS CURRENT AND PREVIOUS RESIDENCES THOROUGHLY AND WERE UNABLE TO UNCOVER ANY EVIDENCE.

YES, I'M SURE ALL OF THE EVIDENCE IS SOMEWHERE AT THE BOTTOM OF THE EAST RIVER BY NOW, ALONG WITH THE ORIGINAL PLANS FOR MY INVENTION.
HE SIMPLY CLEANED UP AFTER HIMSELF.

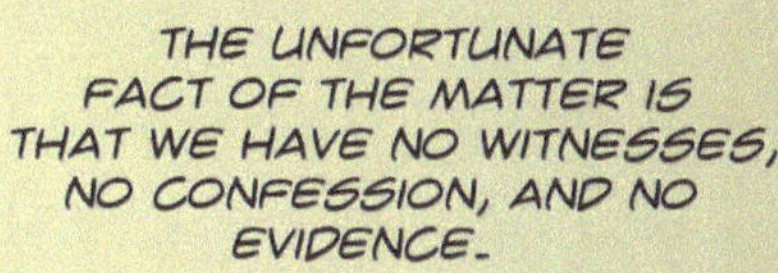

THE UNFORTUNATE FACT OF THE MATTER IS THAT WE HAVE NO WITNESSES, NO CONFESSION, AND NO EVIDENCE.
WE HAVE NOTHING.
AND THE FACT THAT YOUR INVENTION AND HIS ARE SO SIMILAR ALSO MEANS LITTLE. SUCH THINGS HAPPEN. AND, HE HAS ALREADY FILED THE PATENT.
TAKING THIS TO TRIAL WOULD BE FUTILE.

THAT IS WHY UNTIL FURTHER DEVELOPMENTS ARISE I MUST REMOVE MYSELF FROM THIS CASE.
I AM SORRY.

I SEE.

THANK YOU FOR YOUR TIME.

GOOD EVENING SIR.

GOOD EVENING.
I WAS INVITED BY
MISTER MONROE.

MAY I
SEE YOUR
INVITATION
PLEASE?

CERTAINLY.

THANK YOU.
ENJOY YOUR
EVENING SIR.

I SHALL TRY.

EXCUSE ME SIR.

YES?

WOULD YOU LIKE SOMETHING TO DRINK?

YES. ALL RIGHT.

THANK YOU.
ALLOW ME TO INTRODUCE MYSELF.
MY NAME IS LEVI.
MAY I ASK FOR YOUR NAME?
I AM ANASTASIA.

ANASTASIA.
IT IS A PLEASURE TO MEET YOU.

IT IS A PLEASURE TO MEET YOU AS WELL.

AUGUSTUS.
ARE YOU ALIVE?
YES.

MOLLY?

CLICK

HELLO.

HELLO.

MY DEAR MOLLY.

IF YOU CAN HEAR ME, I KNOW THAT YOU WOULD WANT ME TO MOVE FORWARD WITH MY LIFE AND BE HAPPY.

HOWEVER, I HAVE COME TO THE CONCLUSION THAT UNTIL JUSTICE PREVAILS, I WILL NOT BE ABLE TO DO SO.

UNFORTUNATELY, IT APPEARS THAT I WILL NOT BE ABLE TO BUILD A LEGAL CASE AGAINST THE MAN WHO ENDED YOURS AND EMILY'S LIFE, AND WHO HAS CAUSED SO MUCH MISERY IN MY OWN.

AND WHILE I WASTE AWAY IN THIS TORMENTED STATE THAT HAS BEEN INFLICTED UPON ME, I HAVE LEARNED THAT THE MAN WHO IS THE CAUSE OF THIS MISERY IS ENJOYING FAME AND FORTUNE.

IF YOU ARE HERE. IF YOU CAN HEAR ME. I WANT YOU TO KNOW THAT I HAVE LEARNED THAT THE CULPRIT WILL BE APPEARING AT AN EVENT TONIGHT.

I HAVE COME TO THE CONCLUSION THAT THE ONLY WAY TO FIND PEACE IS TO SEE TO IT THAT THIS MAN RECEIVES THE JUSTICE THAT HE HAS THUS FAR ELUDED.
AFTER I ACCOMPLISH THIS, IT WILL BE MY INTENTION TO JOIN YOU AND EMILY IN THE AFTER-LIFE, WHICH I BELIEVE IS THE ONLY WAY OUT OF THIS PREDICAMENT.
UNTIL THAT MOMENT ARRIVES, I WILL CONTINUE TO HOPE AND DREAM OF ONE DAY SEEING YOU AND EMILY AGAIN.

GOOD-BYE FOR NOW . . .
GOODBYE FOR NOW.

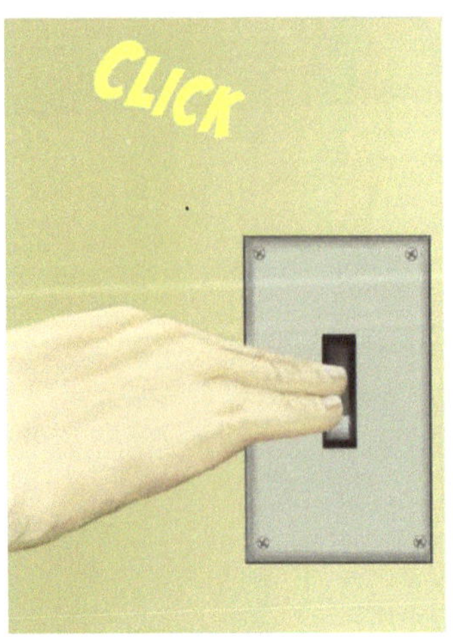

CLICK

KaCHUNK

WHOAH.

EXCUSE ME SIR, BUT YOU LOOK FAMILIAR.
IS YOUR NAME LEVI PICKETT?

IT IS.
YES INDEED. I SAW YOUR PICTURE IN THE HERALD.
CONGRATULATIONS ON YOUR SUCCESS.

THANK YOU VERY MUCH.

I AM CURIOUS WHAT NEW INVENTIONS ARE IN STORE.

I HAVE NOTHING TO REVEAL AT THIS TIME, ALTHOUGH THAT MAY CHANGE BY TOMORROW.

WELL I WISH YOU THE VERY BEST OF LUCK.

THANK YOU VERY MUCH.
GOOD BYE.

PICKETT!

DO YOU KNOW WHO I AM?

I MOST CERTAINLY DO NOT.

I AM THE MAN WHO LOST HIS FAMILY AND HIS HOME BECAUSE OF YOU.

I DON'T KNOW WHAT YOU TALKING ABOUT.

I WANT YOU TO ADMIT WHAT YOU DID IN FRONT OF ALL THESE WITNESSES, AND THEN I WANT YOU TO BEG ME FOR FORGIVENESS.
I WILL GRANT YOU THIS ONE CHANCE TO DO THE RIGHT THING.
DO NOT WASTE IT!

YOU SIR, HAVE CLEARLY LOST YOUR MIND.
GOOD BYE.

YOU HAVE JUST COMMITTED YOUR FINAL MISTAKE.

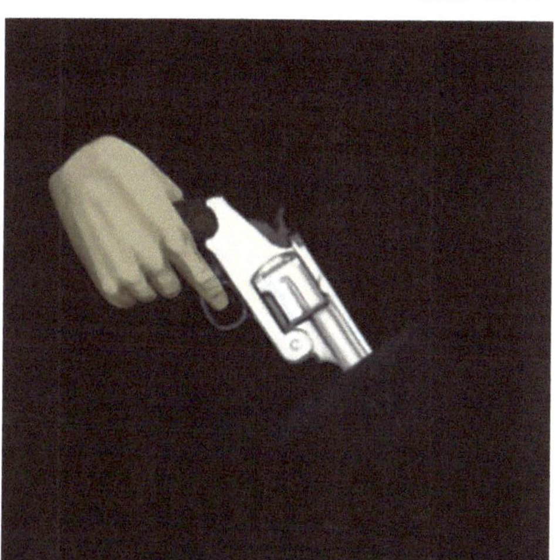

HE HAS A GUN!

BAM

YOU FOOLS! LET GO!

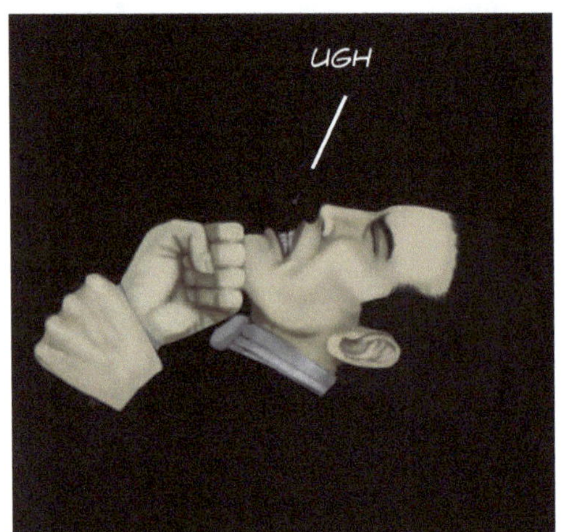

UGH

OOF

LET GO OR I WILL SHOOT!

DO NOT FOLLOW ME!

WAS THAT AUGUSTUS SCOTT?

I DO BELIEVE THAT IT WAS.

MISTER HIRSCHFELD?

YES MISSES BUCHINSKY.

SOMETHING WAS DELIVERED WHILE YOU WERE OUT.
I HAVE BEEN HOLDING IT FOR YOU.

THAT IS ODD.
I WAS NOT EXPECTING A DELIVERY.

HERE YOU ARE.

THANK YOU VERY MUCH.
GOOD NIGHT.

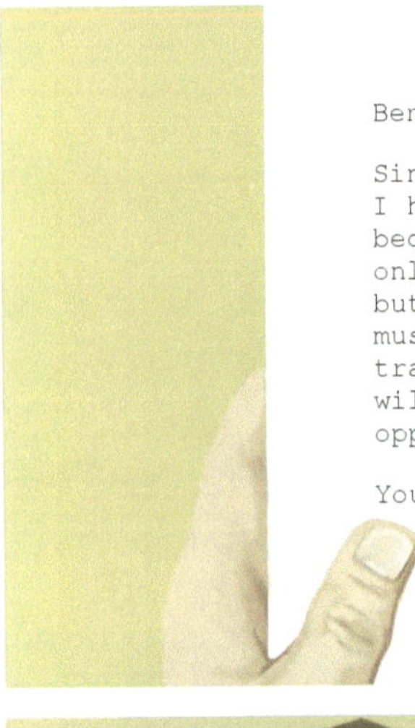

Benny.

Since you are the closest thing to family that
I have left in this world, I have decided to
bequeath to you the remains of my fortune. I
only ask that you use not only for yourself
but for the benefit of humanity. However, you
must know that if circumstances do not
transpire in the manner in which I intend I
will need to reclaim this property when
opportunity permits.

Your friend, Augustus.

LATER THAT NIGHT.
NOK
NOK

CLICK

WHO IS IT?

A FRIEND.

COME IN.

SORRY TO DISTURB YOU AT THIS HOUR, BUT UNFORTUNATELY I CAN ONLY TRAVEL LATE AT NIGHT.

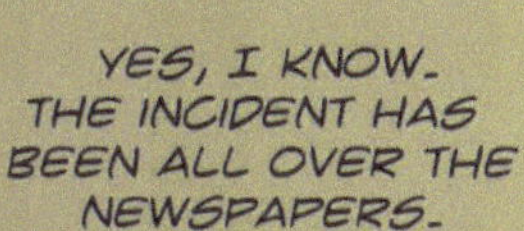

YES, I KNOW. THE INCIDENT HAS BEEN ALL OVER THE NEWSPAPERS.
A REWARD HAS EVEN BEEN OFFERED FOR YOUR CAPTURE.
YOU SHOULD NOT STILL BE IN NEW YORK, OR EVEN AMERICA FOR THAT MATTER.

YES, I REALIZE THAT. BUT I HAVE A MATTER TO ATTEND TO HERE.
A MATTER THAT HAS STILL NOT BEEN RESOLVED.

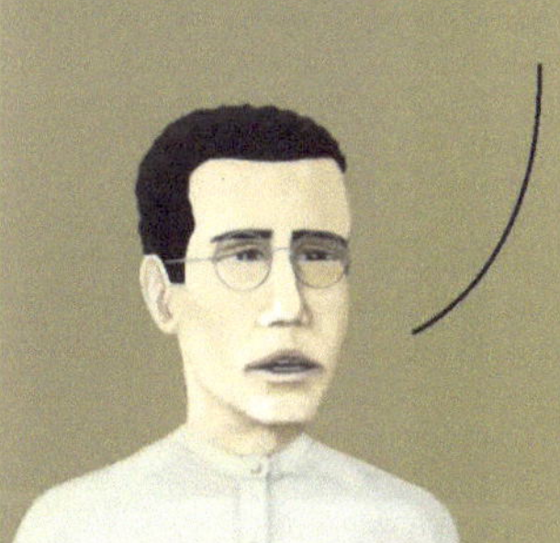

YOU HAVE MADE YOUR POINT.
SOME ARE EVEN WONDERING IF YOU'RE ACCUSATION IS TRUE.
HAVEN'T YOU DONE ENOUGH?

MISTER PICKETT HAS STILL NOT BEEN HELD ACCOUNTABLE FOR HIS CRIMES.
I HAVE NOTHING ELSE TO LIVE FOR BUT TO SEE THAT HE IS BROUGHT TO JUSTICE.
IN ORDER TO DO THIS, I REQUIRE SOME HELP.

I AM HERE TO ASK FOR HELP.
BENNY . . . WILL YOU HELP ME?

OH NO.

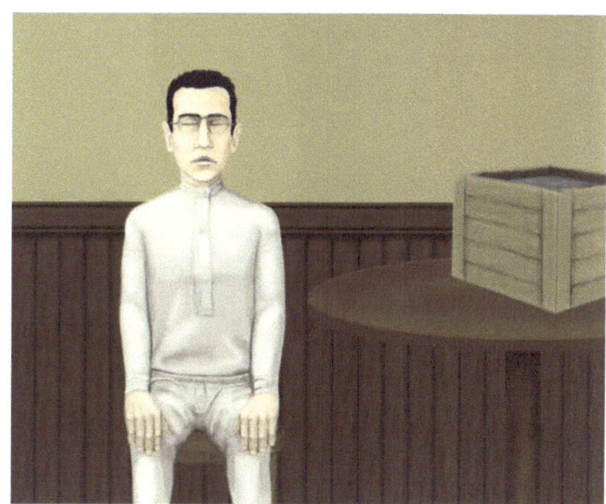

- - - SINCE YOU LET ME GO I HAVE BEEN UNABLE TO FIND SUITABLE EMPLOYMENT.

IF I WERE TO ACCEPT YOUR REQUEST, WOULD I BE CONSIDERED REEMPLOYED?

ABSOLUTELY. I WILL EVEN INCREASE YOUR COMPENSATION BY A SUBSTANTIAL AMOUNT.
A VERY SUBSTANTIAL AMOUNT.

- - - ALL RIGHT.

THANK YOU MY FRIEND.
THANK YOU.

SO WHAT IS YOUR PLAN?

TO BEGIN WITH, A DISCRETE WORK-SPACE IS REQUIRED.

ALL RIGHT.
I WILL BEGIN LOOKING FIRST THING IN THE MORNING.

EXCELLENT.
THE LESS THAT YOU KNOW THE BETTER, SO THAT IS ALL THAT I AM GOING TO SAY FOR NOW.

BY THE WAY, DO YOU HAVE ANYTHING IN YOUR TOOL COLLECTION THAT WOULD HELP ME PICK A LOCK?

I PROBABLY DO. WHY?

THE LESS YOU KNOW THE BETTER.

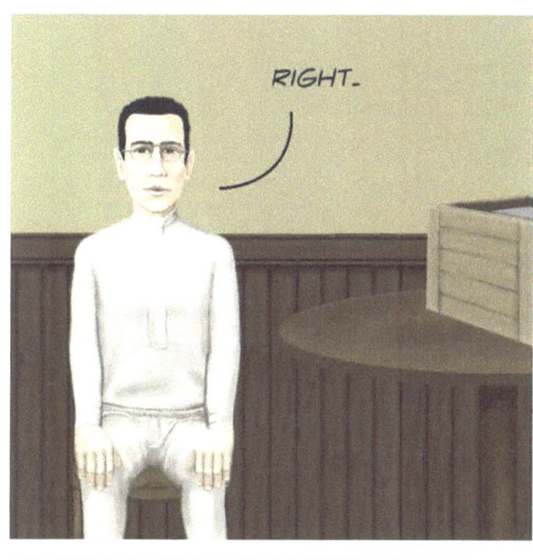

RIGHT.

TWO WIRES SHOULD DO IT.
THANK YOU.

I SUPPOSE THAT YOU WILL BE NEEDING THIS BACK.

DO ME A FAVOR.
I CANNOT TRAVEL AROUND WITH THAT.
PLEASE RETAIN IT FOR ME FOR THE TIME BEING.
I KNOW I CAN TRUST YOU.

OF COURSE YOU CAN.

ALL RIGHT.
GOOD NIGHT FOR NOW MY FRIEND.

AND ONE MORE THING.
I WANT YOU TO KNOW THAT NONE OF THIS IS ABOUT REVENGE.
IT IS ABOUT JUSTICE.

I KNOW THAT YOU ARE NOT A COMMON RUFFIAN.
I MAY NOT COMPLETELY AGREE WITH WHAT YOU ARE DOING, BUT . . .
I UNDERSTAND.

KACHUNK.

220

NOK
NOK
HELLO?
ANYONE HOME?

CLICK
CLICK
CLICK
CLICK
CLICK

CLICK
CLICK
CLICK
CLICK
CHOK

CREEEEEEEEEEK

CLICK

THAK   THAK   THAK

RYE
Bourbon Whiskey
H.B. Kirk &
D CROW

SO MISTER
PICKETT.
YOU WANTED
OUT OF HERE.
I UNDERSTAND.

DO YOU LIKE THE MUSIC?
YES, WHAT IS IT?
IT IS FREDERIC CHOPIN'S NOCTURNE IN E FLAT MAJOR.
IT IS BEING PLAYED ON A STEAM-POWERED GRAMOPHONE.
IT IS A LITTLE IMPROVEMENT THAT I MADE TO BERLINER'S INVENTION.

GRAMOPHONE? I THOUGHT IT WAS CALLED A PHONOGRAPH?

A PHONOGRAPH PLAYS SHORT RECORDED EMBOSSINGS OFF OF A CYLINDER.
THE GRAMOPHONE, HOWEVER, IS A HIGHER QUALITY MACHINE THAT PLAYS SOUND ETCHINGS OFF OF A DISK.
I MUST CONFESS TO BEING A LITTLE JEALOUS OF THE MAN WHO INVENTED IT.

WOULD YOU LIKE SOME TEA?
YES, THANK YOU . . . SO TELL ME, DO YOU THINK THAT AUGUSTUS SCOTT WILL TRY TO MAKE ANOTHER ATTEMPT ON YOUR LIFE?

THAT IS A POSSIBILITY.
HE MAY EVEN TRY TO FIND ME HERE, HOWEVER, WE HAVE NO REASON TO BE ALARMED.
NOT ONLY HAVE I ALREADY INSTALLED BARS ON ALL THE WINDOWS AND LOCKS ON ALL THE DOORS, AND NOT ONLY AM I IN THE PROCESS OF HIRING GUARDS, BUT I HAVE BEEN DEVISING MY OWN SECURITY SYSTEM.

YOUR OWN SECURITY SYSTEM?

YES. I HAVE BEEN CONCEIVING NEW INVENTIONS THAT WILL AVERT ANY ONE ATTEMPTING TO TRESPASS UPON THIS PROPERTY.
IN FACT, A TEAM OF LABORERS WILL BE ARRIVING ON MONDAY TO HELP ME WITH THE CONSTRUCTION OF SOME OF THESE CONTRAPTIONS.
THEN OF COURSE, ANYONE ATTEMPTING TO TRESPASS WILL ALSO HAVE TO CONTEND WITH THE ELECTRO—GUN AS WELL, WHICH REMINDS ME. I AM TARGET PRACTICING TOMORROW.
WOULD YOU LIKE TO JOIN ME?

MAY I SHOOT THE ELECTRO—GUN?

OF COURSE YOU CAN.

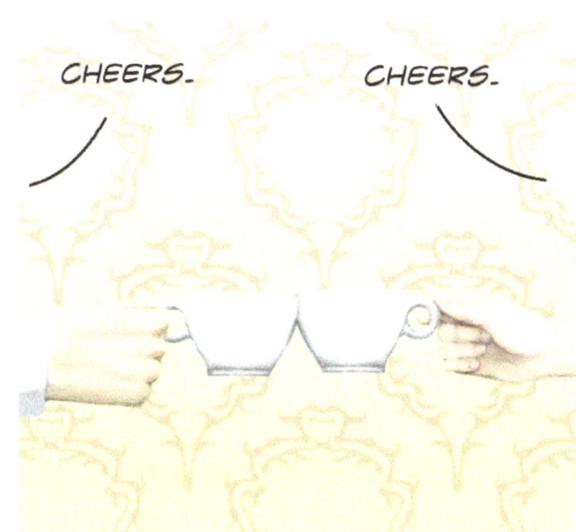

CHEERS.
CHEERS.

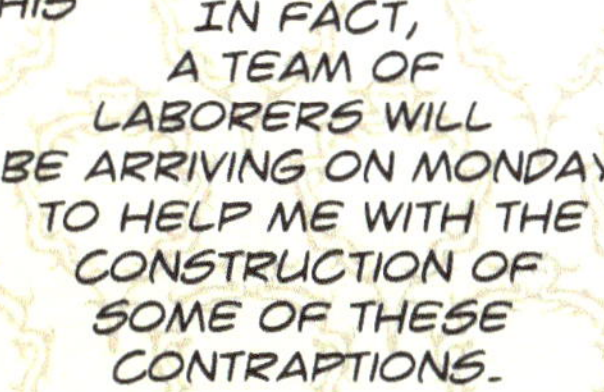

HELLO.

DAMN!
YOU STARTLED ME.

I'M SORRY, BUT UNTIL I KNOW THAT YOU ARE ALONE I MUST CONCEAL MYSELF.

RIGHT.
SO WHAT DO YOU THINK OF THIS PLACE?

THIS PLACE WILL DO JUST FINE.
THANK YOU FOR YOUR WORK.

YOU'RE WELCOME.
SO WHAT'S NEXT?

HERE, THIS IS A LIST OF ALL OF THE MATERIALS THAT ARE REQUIRED.
AND HERE IS SOME MONEY.

ALL RIGHT, BUT THIS MIGHT TAKE ME AN ENTIRE DAY.

WELL THEN, I GUESS YOU HAD BETTER GET STARTED.

WHAT IS
THE MATTER?

ARE YOU
REALLY SURE
ABOUT TRYING TO
MAKE ANOTHER ATTEMPT
ON PICKETT'S LIFE?
BECAUSE IF SO,
SURELY YOU MUST
REALIZE THAT UNLIKE
LAST TIME, NEXT TIME
HE WILL BE EXPECTING
YOU.

YES.
I REALIZE
THAT.

AS LONG AS
YOU ARE STILL
ON THE LOOSE IT IS
UNLIKELY THAT HE WILL
MAKE ANY MORE PUBLIC
APPEARANCES.
WHAT ARE
YOU GOING TO
DO? GO TO HIS
HOUSE?

YES, AS
A MATTER OF
FACT.
THAT IS
PRECISELY
WHAT I INTEND
TO DO.

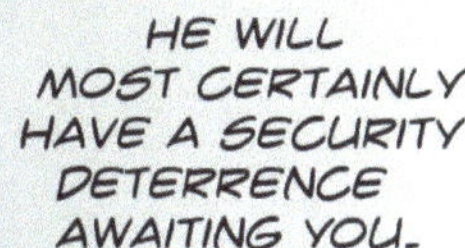

HE WILL
MOST CERTAINLY
HAVE A SECURITY
DETERRENCE
AWAITING YOU.

IN THAT CASE,
I WILL JUST NEED
TO MAKE SURE THAT
I WILL BE ABLE TO
OVERCOME HIS
DETERRENCE.

BENNY,
LISTEN TO ME.
THIS WILL NOT
ONLY COME DOWN
TO A BATTLE OF WEAPONS,
BUT OF MINDS, AND I AM
THE SMARTER MAN.
NOW PLEASE
BE A GOOD FELLOW
AND GET STARTED ON THAT
LIST BEFORE THE DAY
GETS AWAY FROM US.

KACHUNK

SO WHAT
IS THIS GOING
TO BE?

A TRAP
DOOR OR
SOMETHING?

YES.

HERE IS YOUR BODY ARMOR.
I HOPE YOU LIKE IT.

I DO LIKE IT.
I AM SURPRISED THAT YOU WENT TO SUCH EXTRA LENGTHS TO GIVE IT SUCH ARTISTIC FLAIR.

I HAVE TO FEEL PROUD OF WHAT I DO IN ORDER TO ENJOY IT, AND I MUST ADMIT THAT I AM FEELING QUITE PROUD OF THAT.

FINE JOB. FINE JOB INDEED.

AND NOW, I HAVE SOMETHING TO SHOW YOU.

WHAT IS THAT?

THIS IS A FOREARM-MOUNTED PNEUMATIC FORCE WEAPON.

IT FIRES A SMALL PROJECTILE THAT IS LOADED INTO IT.

ITS GREATEST ATTRIBUTE IS THAT IT IS SILENT.
I WILL THEREFORE BE ABLE TO USE THIS WITHOUT ALERTING THE ENTIRE NEIGHBORHOOD.

LET'S NOW PUT THIS INVENTION AND THE BODY ARMOR TO THE TEST.

YOU MAY WANT TO STAND BACK.

ALL RIGHT.
HERE IT GOES.

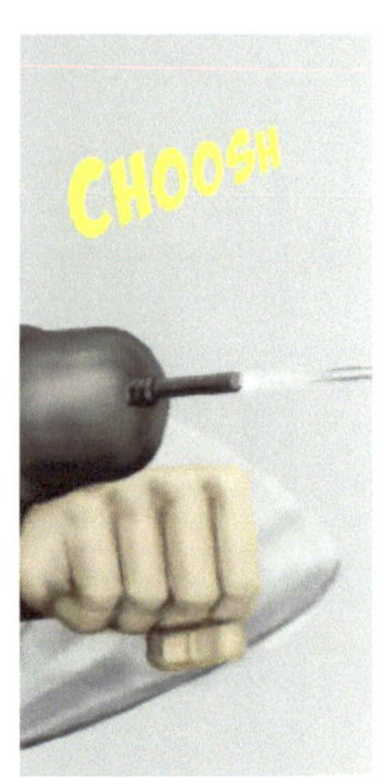

CHOOSH

CLANGK

IMPRESSIVE.

I AM JUST GETTING STARTED.

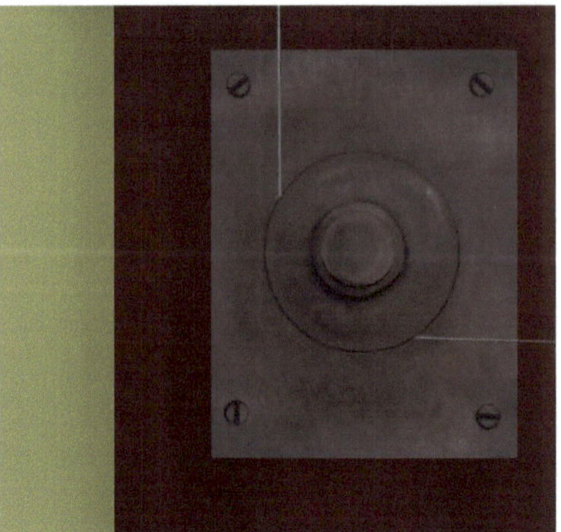

CHIK
WOOOOOSH

HA HA
HA HA
HA HAAA!

HEY
AUGUSTUS!

COME AND
GET IT!

DO NOT
BE ALARMED.
IT IS
ONLY ME.

I KNEW THAT
IT WAS YOU.
I COULD
TELL BY THE
FOOT STEPS.

I HAVE
OBTAINED THE
CHLORINE.

THANK YOU.
JUST PUT IT OVER
THERE ON THE FLOOR
FOR NOW, AND PLEASE BE
CAREFUL WHEN YOU SET IT
DOWN. IF THAT GLASS
CONTAINER WERE TO
BREAK IT WOULD
RUIN THE DAY.

WHAT ARE
YOU GOING TO DO
WITH ALL OF THIS
CHLORINE?

I AM GOING TO
MAKE GAS BOMBS
WITH IT.

GAS BOMBS?

YES, BUT
WE WILL GET TO
THAT LATER.

NOW, LET
ME SHOW YOU
WHAT THIS DEVICE
CAN DO.

IS THAT
THE FLAME-
SHOOTER THAT YOU
HAVE BEEN TELLING
ME ABOUT?

CHIK

WOOOSH

YES IT IS.

WELL THAT
IS CREATIVE.

I WONDER
HOW MISTER PICKETT
WILL LIKE HAVING HIS
HOME BURNED DOWN?

CHUG
CHUG
CHUG
CHUG
CHUG

SSSHHHHHHHHHHHHH

I MISSED YOU.
I MISSED YOU TOO.

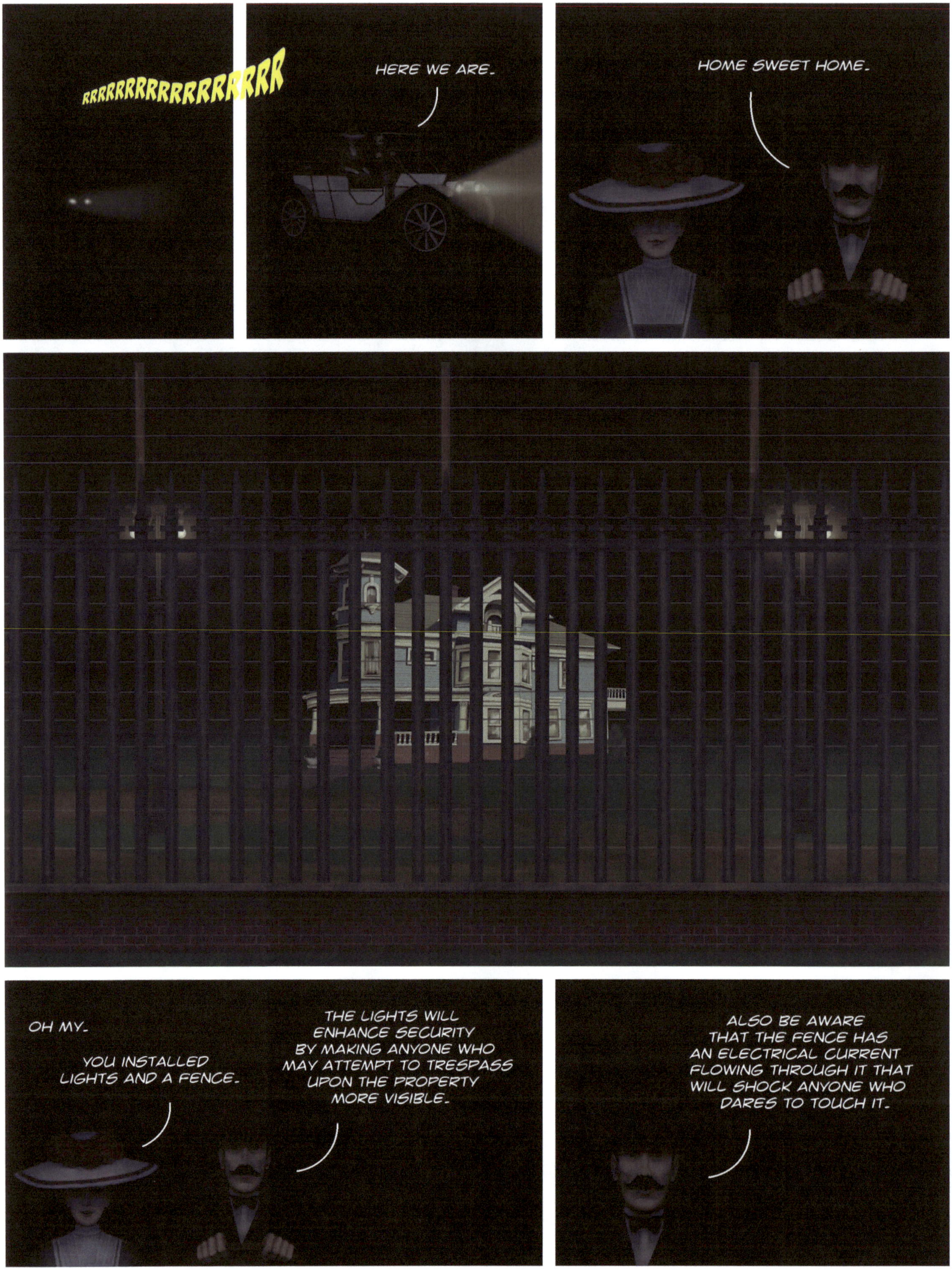

RRRRRRRRRRRRRRR

HERE WE ARE.

HOME SWEET HOME.

OH MY.

YOU INSTALLED LIGHTS AND A FENCE.

THE LIGHTS WILL ENHANCE SECURITY BY MAKING ANYONE WHO MAY ATTEMPT TO TRESPASS UPON THE PROPERTY MORE VISIBLE.

ALSO BE AWARE THAT THE FENCE HAS AN ELECTRICAL CURRENT FLOWING THROUGH IT THAT WILL SHOCK ANYONE WHO DARES TO TOUCH IT.

AND NOW THERE IS SOMEONE WHO I WOULD LIKE TO INTRODUCE YOU TO.

ANASTASIA, THIS IS FRANCO.
HE WILL BE OVERSEEING SECURITY ON THE NIGHT-SHIFT.

HELLO FRANCO.

HELLO.

FRANCO IS A FORMER ARMY SOLDIER AND CHAMPION BARE-KNUCKLE PRIZE-FIGHTER.
HE COULD RIP A MAN IN TWO WITH HIS BARE HANDS IF HE WANTED TO.
ISN'T THAT RIGHT?

IT'S TRUE.

HAHA
WELL THAT IS GOOD TO KNOW.

ALL RIGHT. LET'S LET FRANCO GET BACK TO WORK.
I HAVE SOMETHING ELSE TO SHOW YOU.

GOOD BYE.
KEEP US SAFE.
I WILL.

RRRRRRRRRRRRR

WHERE ARE WE GOING?
YOU ARE ABOUT TO FIND OUT.

OH MY.

WELCOME TO THE GARDEN OF LIGHTS!
IT'S WONDERFUL!

I LOVE IT!

WHEN YOU WERE GONE I REALIZED HOW MUCH YOU MEAN TO ME.

I REALIZED THAT I NEVER WANT TO BE WITHOUT YOU.

ANASTASIA GIROUX . . . I LOVE YOU.
WILL YOU MARRY ME?

YES.
YES I WILL MARRY YOU!

THIS MIGHT BE IT.
RRRRRRRRRR

SLOW DOWN BUT DON'T STOP.

THIS IS DEFINITELY IT.
JUST KEEP GOING FOR NOW.

WE NEED TO FIND A PLACE TO PARK DOWN THE ROAD SO THAT WE CAN GET A BETTER LOOK ON FOOT.

THERE ARE LAMPS ALL OVER THE YARD.
DURING THE NIGHT THIS PLACE MUST BE LIT UP.
YES.
THAT IS UNFORTUNATE.

WHAT DO YOU THINK THAT THE WIRES BEHIND THE BARS ARE FOR?
DO YOU SEE THOSE SMALL WHITE OBJECTS ATTACHED TO WOODEN POST THAT ARE ALSO ATTACHED TO THE WIRES?

ARE THOSE INSULATORS?

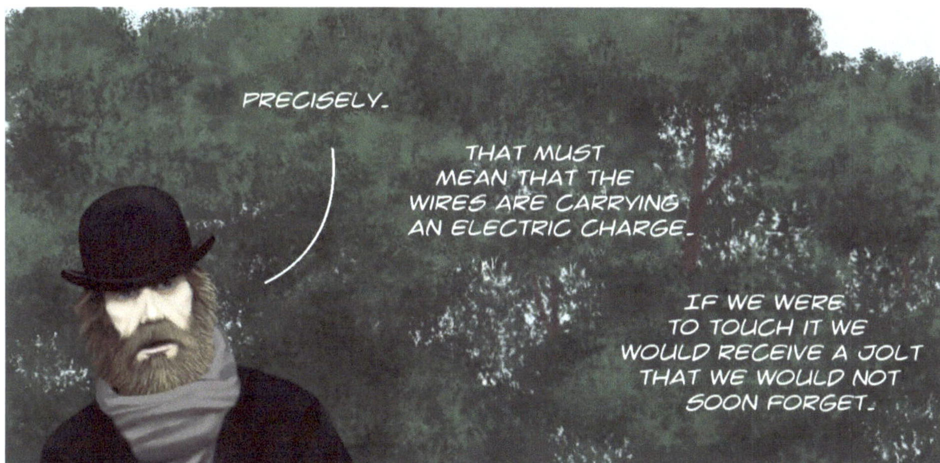

PRECISELY.
THAT MUST MEAN THAT THE WIRES ARE CARRYING AN ELECTRIC CHARGE.
IF WE WERE TO TOUCH IT WE WOULD RECEIVE A JOLT THAT WE WOULD NOT SOON FORGET.

THIS ENDEAVOR IS GOING TO BE EVEN MORE DIFFICULT THAN I ORIGINALLY THOUGHT.

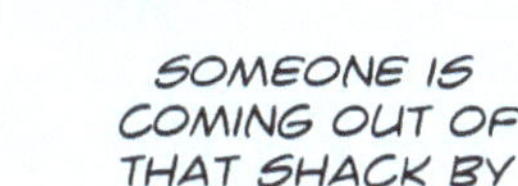

LOOK.

SOMEONE IS COMING OUT OF THAT SHACK BY THE GATE.

WELL, THAT IS CERTAINLY NOT PICKETT.

IT APPEARS TO BE A GUARD STARTING A PATROL.

WE HAD BETTER RETREAT BEFORE WE ARE NOTICED.

SO, HOW ARE YOU GOING TO GET IN?

THAT IS A QUESTION THAT I DO NOT HAVE AN ANSWER TO JUST YET.

I WILL JUST HAVE TO CONCEIVE A WAY TO SURMOUNT THE GATE AND DISABLE THE GUARD.
OR PERHAPS THERE IS SOME WAY TO DISABLE THE GUARD FIRST.

EVEN IF YOU COULD DEFEAT THE GUARD FIRST HOW WOULD YOU SURMOUNT THE GATE?

I DON'T KNOW YET.

I KNOW HOW YOU COULD GET OVER THE FENCE.

HOW?

YOU COULD SIMPLY FLY OVER IT.

THAT MAY ACTUALLY WORK.

KA CHUNK

WHAT ARE YOU DOING?

YOU ARE JUST IN TIME MY DEAR.
I AM ABOUT TO THROW THIS ROCK ONTO THE FLOOR, WHICH SHOULD TRIGGER A PRESSURE SENSITIVE MECHANISM THAT I HAVE INSTALLED.

THE WEIGHT SHOULD TRIGGER THE FIREARM THAT I HAVE MOUNTED INSIDE THE WALL RIGHT HERE.

BUT DO NOT WORRY.
THERE WILL BE A SAFETY SWITCH THAT WILL PREVENT IT FROM GOING OFF WHEN I DO NOT WANT IT TO.
I WILL BE ABLE TO ARM IT AND DISARM IT AT WILL.

YES, ALL RIGHT.

NOW, IF EVERYTHING WORKS AS IT SHOULD, YOU SHOULD HEAR WHAT SOUNDS LIKE A GUN FIRING, BUT DO NOT WORRY.
IT WILL NOT BE AN ACTUAL BULLET, BUT RATHER ONLY A BLANK CARTRIDGE . . .
FOR NOW, THAT IS.
SO YOU MAY WANT TO COVER YOUR EARS.

ALL RIGHT. LET'S GIVE IT A TRY.

BOK

BAM

NOW WE DO NOT HAVE TO WORRY ABOUT ANYONE SNEAKING UP ON US WHEN WE ARE ASLEEP.

YOU ARE A GENIUS.

GOOD MORNING.

GOOD MORNING.

WHAT ARE YOU DOING?

I AM BUILDING MY STRENGTH - - -

IN CASE MY CONFRONTATION WITH MISTER PICKETT DEVOLVES INTO HAND TO HAND COMBAT.

I SEE.
WELL YOU SHOULD KNOW THAT I HAVE THE ITEM THAT YOU REQUESTED.

YOU HAVE
THE TURKEY?

I HAVE
THE TURKEY.

EXCELLENT.

GO AHEAD
AND PUT IT ON
THE TABLE WHILE
I PREPARE.

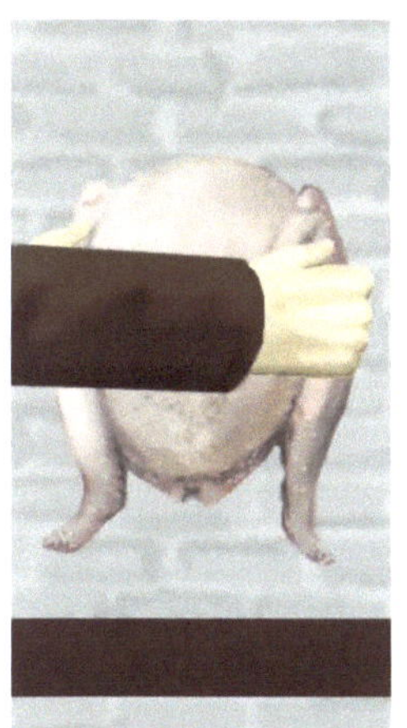

LET'S GIVE
IT A TRY.

CHOOF

FAK

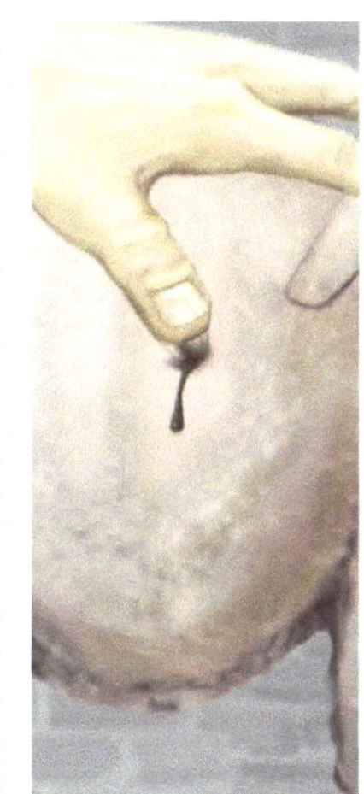

THE OPIUM
HAS INJECTED
INTO THE MEAT.

ONCE AGAIN
YOU HAVE
SUCCEEDED.

WELL MY FRIEND,
IT APPEARS THAT
WE ARE NOW READY TO
PROCEED TO THE FINAL
STAGE OF THIS
ADVENTURE.

LEVI

I AM GOING TO BED.

I WILL BE RIGHT UP MY DEAR.

CLICK

ARE YOU READY TO BE CONNECTED TO THE BALLOONS?

I AM.

DO YOU HAVE THE GAS MASK?

RIGHT HERE.

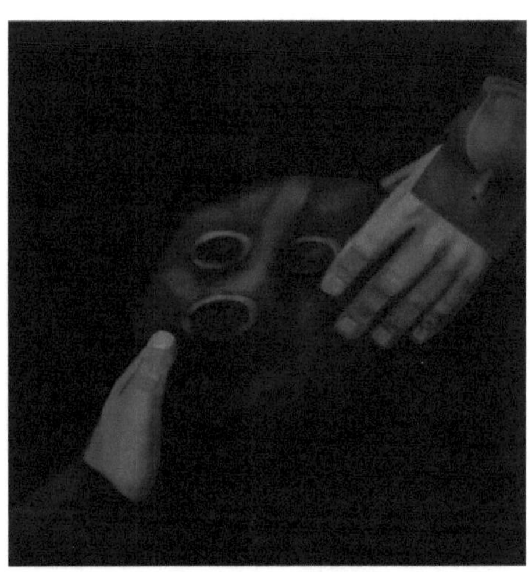

IS SOMETHING WRONG?

YES.
YES THERE IS.

I AM FEELING SCARED OUT OF MY WITS RIGHT NOW.

THIS IS IT BENNY.

TONIGHT SOMEONE'S LIFE MAY COME TO AN END, AND IT JUST MIGHT BE MY OWN.

YOU DON'T HAVE TO DO THIS.

IT'S NOT TOO LATE.

YOU CAN STILL WALK AWAY.

AND LET HIM GET AWAY WITH IT?

AUGUSTUS, LISTEN TO ME.

FOR THE REST OF HIS LIFE HE WILL HAVE TO LIVE WITH THE DARK CLOUD OF GUILT HANGING OVER HIS HEAD.

HE WILL CONSTANTLY HAVE TO LOOK OVER HIS SHOULDER, WONDERING IF YOU WILL BE THERE TO ADMINISTER THE RETRIBUTION THAT HE MUST FEAR IS COMING.

AND IF THERE IS SUCH A PLACE AS A HELL, HE WILL HAVE THAT TO CONTEND WITH ON HIS JUDGMENT DAY.

CAN'T THAT BE ENOUGH?

YOU STILL HAVE MONEY.
YOU CAN STILL LEAVE ALL OF THIS BEHIND AND START A NEW LIFE SOMEPLACE FAR AWAY AND START AGAIN.

AND DO WHAT?

YOU WILL FIND SOMETHING.
IT IS ONLY A MATTER OF OPTIMISM.

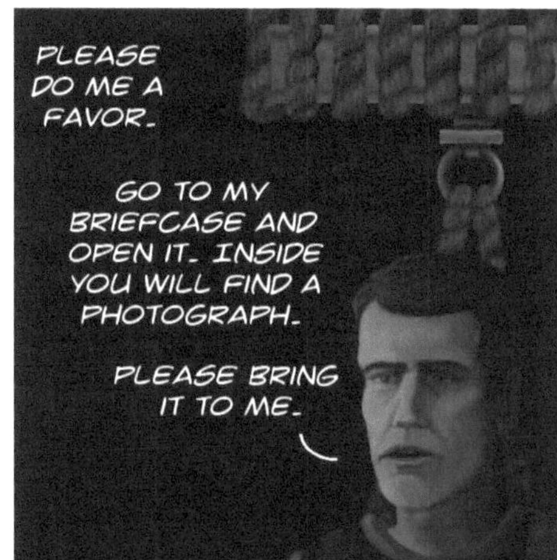
PLEASE DO ME A FAVOR.
GO TO MY BRIEFCASE AND OPEN IT. INSIDE YOU WILL FIND A PHOTOGRAPH.
PLEASE BRING IT TO ME.

LET'S DO ONE LAST WIND TEST.

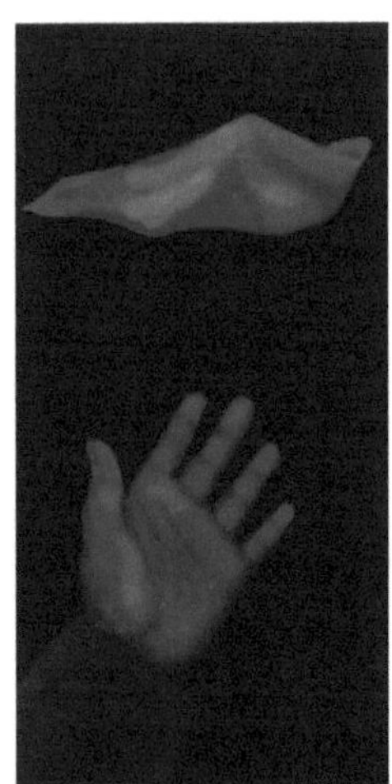

IT'S STILL BLOWING WESTWARD.

THE WIND IS STILL IN OUR FAVOR.
THAT IS A GOOD OMEN DON'T YOU THINK?

I SUPPOSE IT IS.

IT IS NOW ALMOST A HALF PAST TWO.
WE SHALL COMMENCE THE ATTACK AT THREE O'CLOCK.

I HAD BETTER GET GOING THEN.

YES YOU SHOULD.

GOOD LUCK AUGUSTUS.

GOOD LUCK TO YOU AS WELL AND THANK YOU FOR EVERYTHING THAT YOU HAVE DONE FOR ME.

KRSHH
KRSHH
SCRASH

CLICK
RRRRRRRRRRRRRR
WELL AUGUSUTUS . . .
IT'S TOO LATE TO BE A COWARD NOW.
WHAK

RRRRRSHHHHHHHHHHHHHHH

RRRRRRRRSSSSSSHHHHHHHHHHHHHHH

RRRRRRSHHHHHH

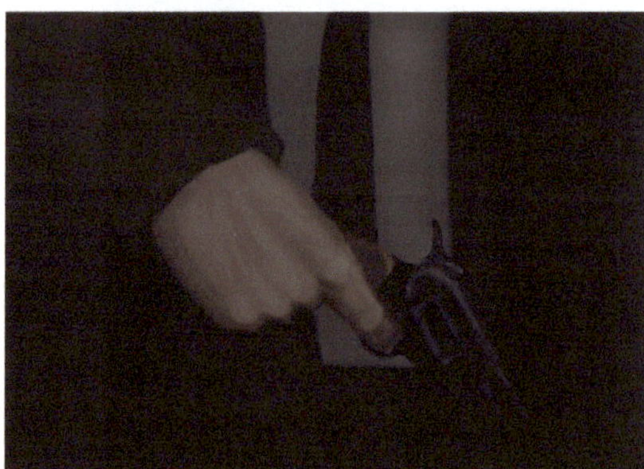

JRRRRRRRSSSSSSSHHHHHH

HUH_

THWACK

THWACK

CLANK

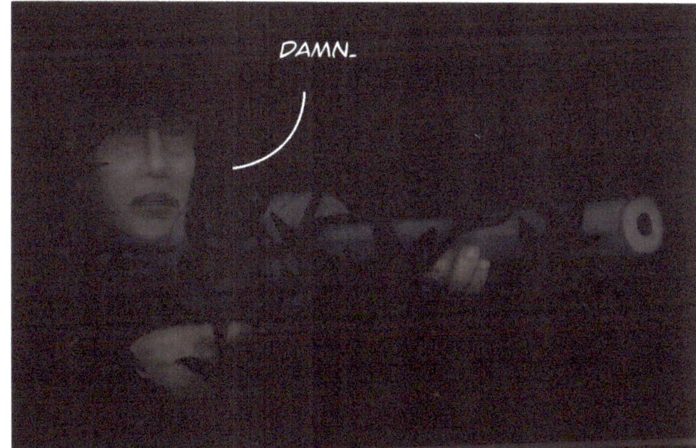DAMN_

WHERE ARE YOU?

JRSHHHHHH

THWACK

THWACK
THWACK
SSSSSSSSSSSHHHHHHHHHHHHHHHHHHHHHHHHHHH

I DO NOT WANT TO SHOOT YOU.
JUST LET GO OF YOUR GUN AND YOU WILL LIVE.

NOW TURN OVER ONTO YOUR STOMACH AND PUT YOUR HANDS BEHIND YOUR BACK.

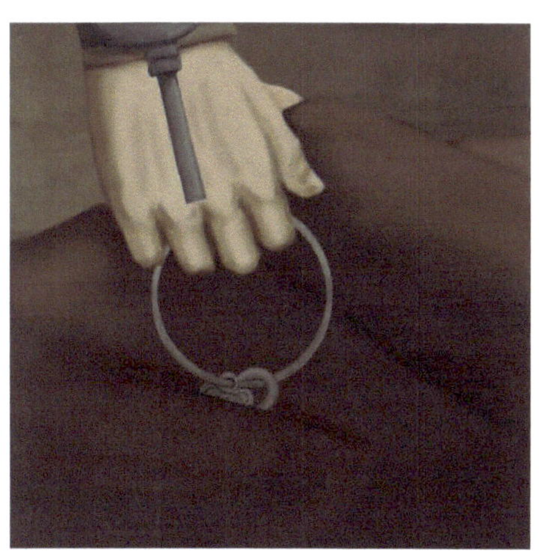

IS ONE OF THESE THE KEYS TO THE HOUSE?

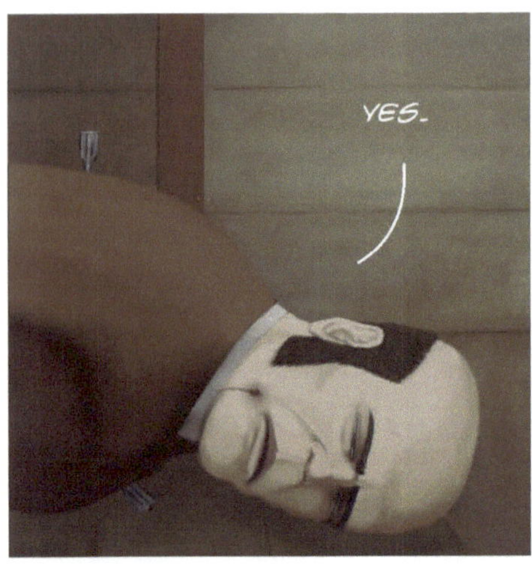

YES.

IS ANYONE ELSE IN THE HOUSE OTHER THAN PICKETT?

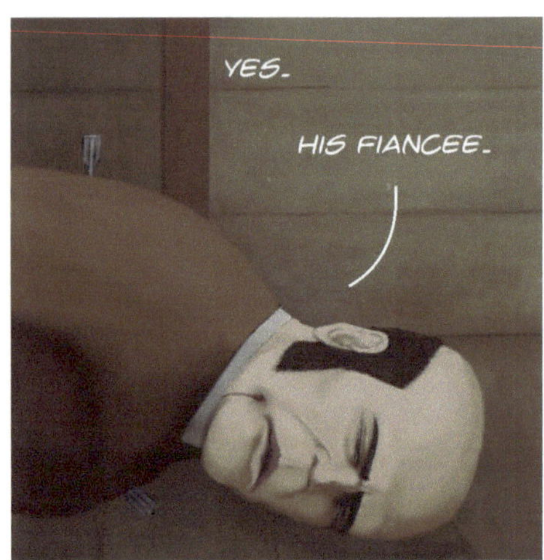

YES.
HIS FIANCEE.

WHERE ARE THEY RIGHT NOW?

UPSTAIRS BEDROOM AT THE END OF THE HALL.
UNLESS HE IS STILL DOWNSTAIRS.

WHERE DOWNSTAIRS?

HE SOMETIMES STAYS UP LATE TO READ IN HIS STUDY.

WHERE IS THE STUDY?

IT'S ON THE LEFT SIDE.
BEHIND THE PARLOR.
IN THE BACK.

THANK YOU FOR YOUR COOPERATION.
ALL THAT YOU HAVE TO DO NOW IS TO RELAX AND ENJOY THE REST OF YOUR SHIFT.

GOOD NIGHT.

NOBODY WATCHING IN THE WINDOWS.

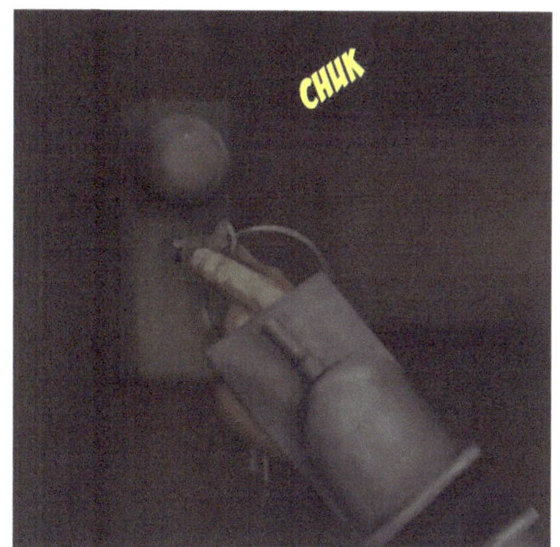

CHUK

CREEEEK
CREEEK
GO.

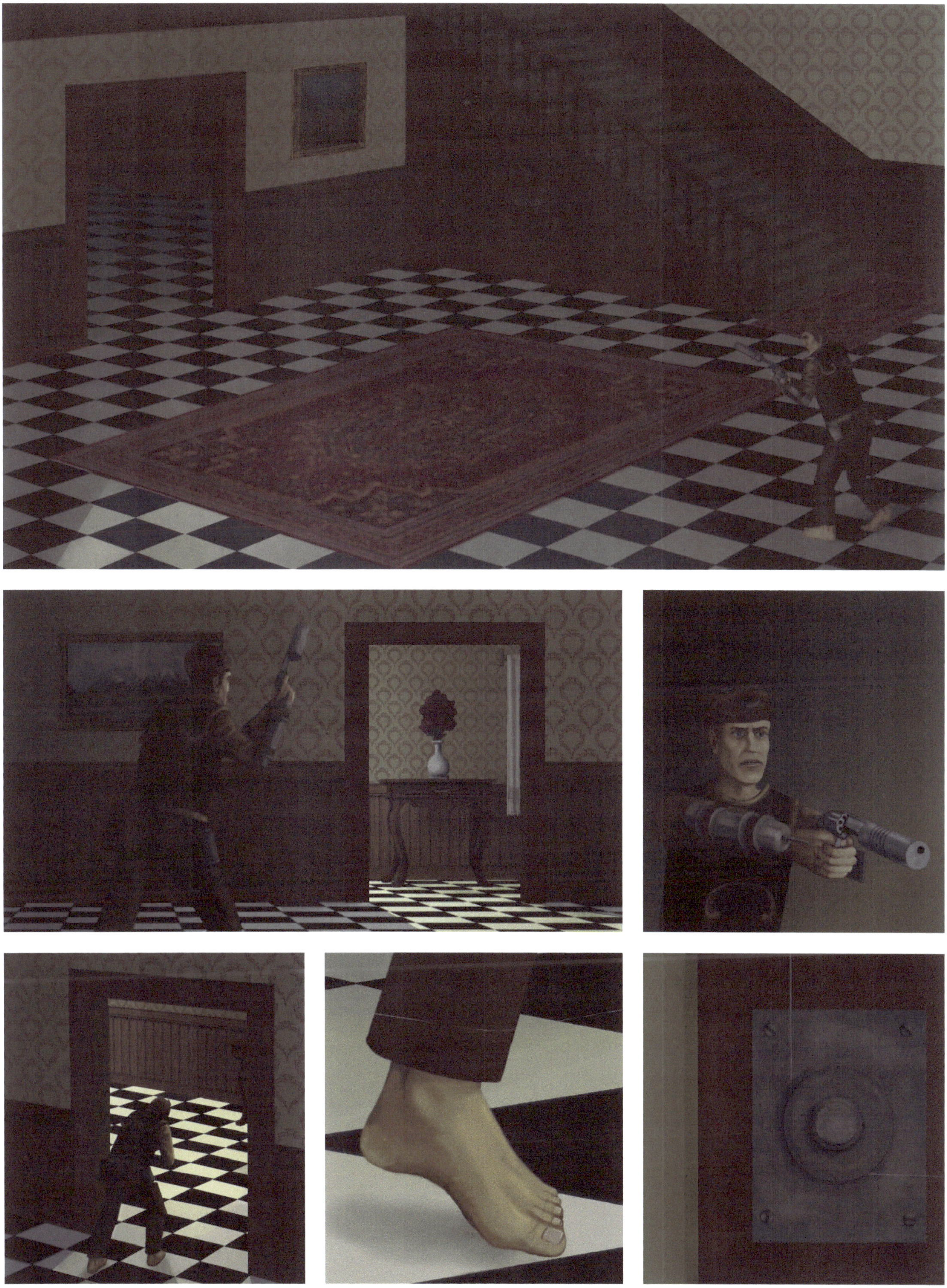

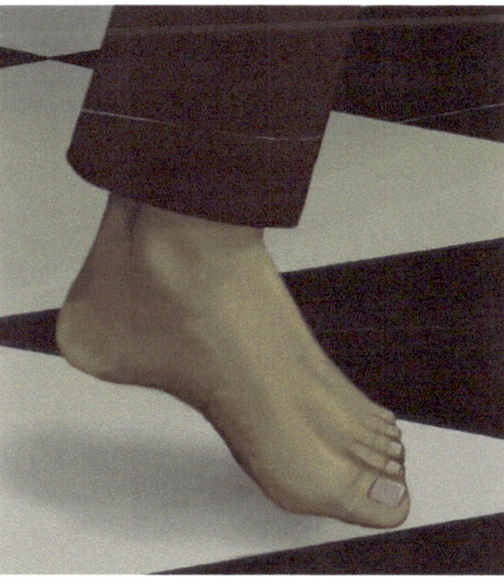

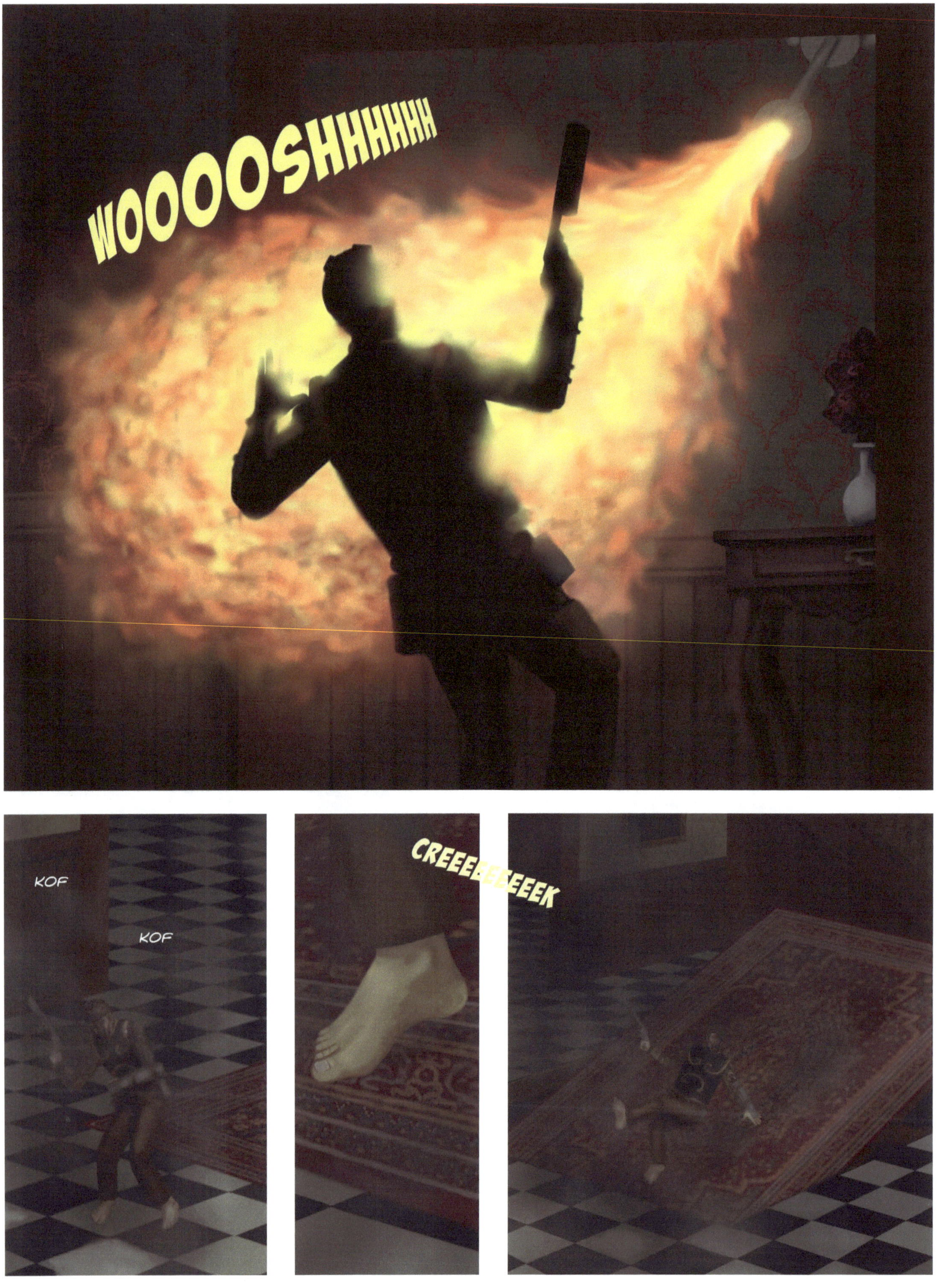

WOOOOSHHHHH

KOF
KOF

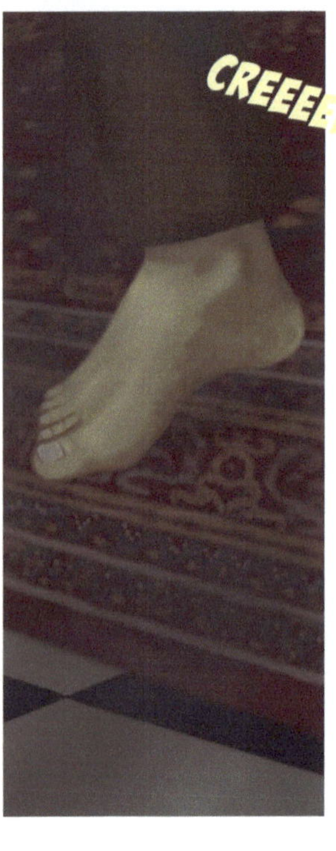
CREEEEEEEEEK

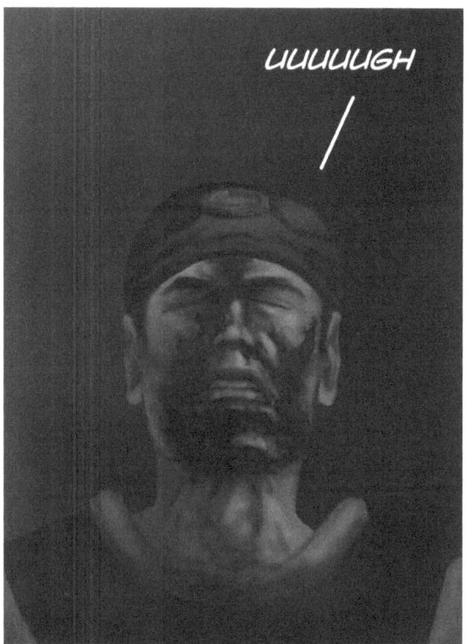
UUUUUGH

GREETINGS MISTER SCOTT.
I HAVE BEEN EXPECTING YOU.

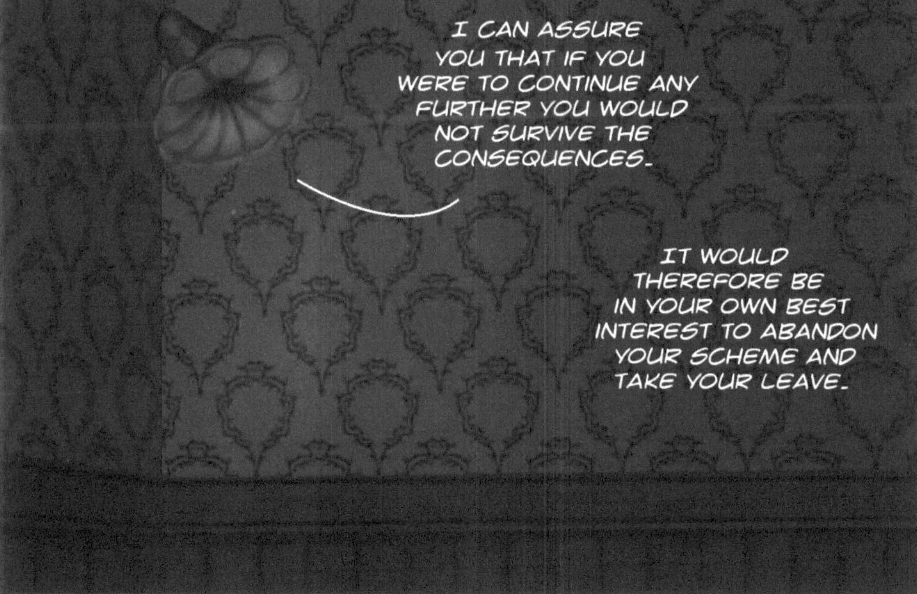
I CAN ASSURE YOU THAT IF YOU WERE TO CONTINUE ANY FURTHER YOU WOULD NOT SURVIVE THE CONSEQUENCES.
IT WOULD THEREFORE BE IN YOUR OWN BEST INTEREST TO ABANDON YOUR SCHEME AND TAKE YOUR LEAVE.

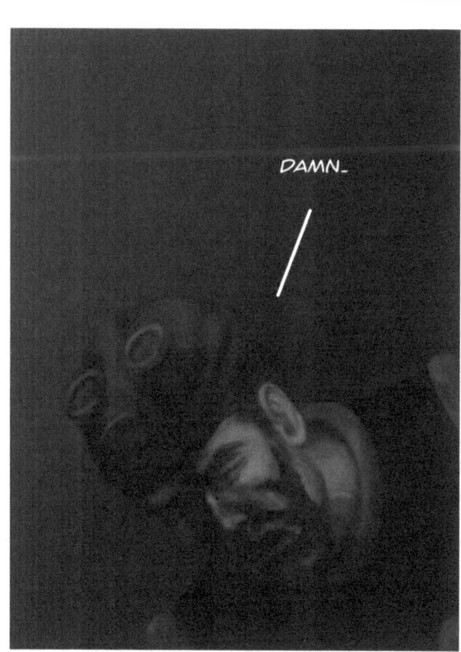
DAMN.

CREEEEEK

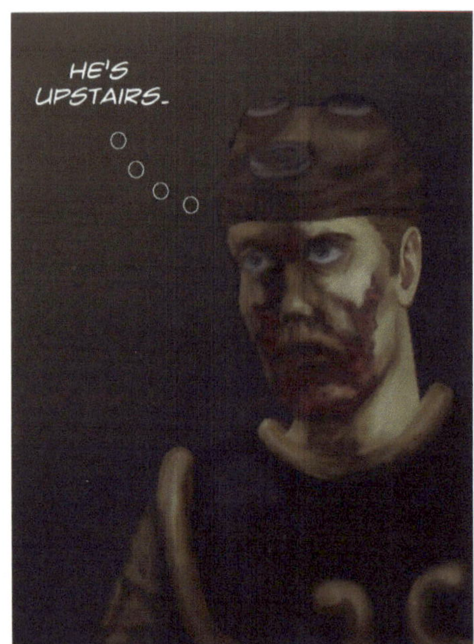

HE'S UPSTAIRS.

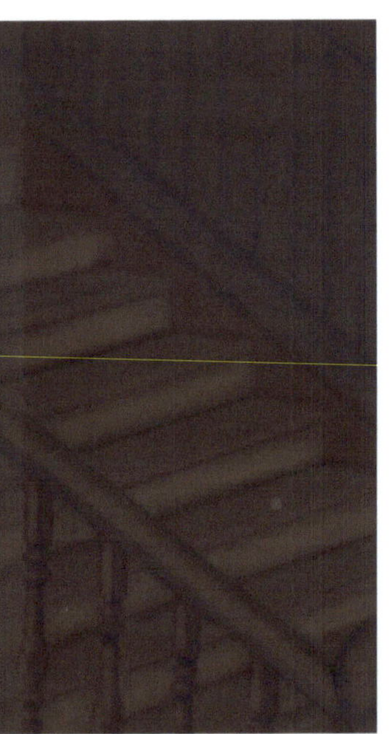

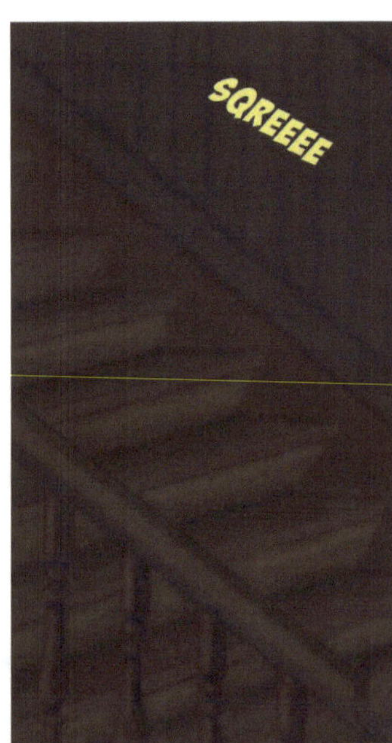

SQREEEE

CHOK

CLUNK

KACHUNK

DO NOT STEP
ON THE CARPET.
NOW USE THE
FLAME SHOOTER TO
SMOKE THEM OUT.

BAM
BAM
BAM

BAM
BAM
CLANK

CHUK
CHUK
CHUK
CHUK
CHUK
CHUK

CLICK

OUT OF BULLETS!

BAM
UGH!

I'M HIT!
GET OUT OF HERE!

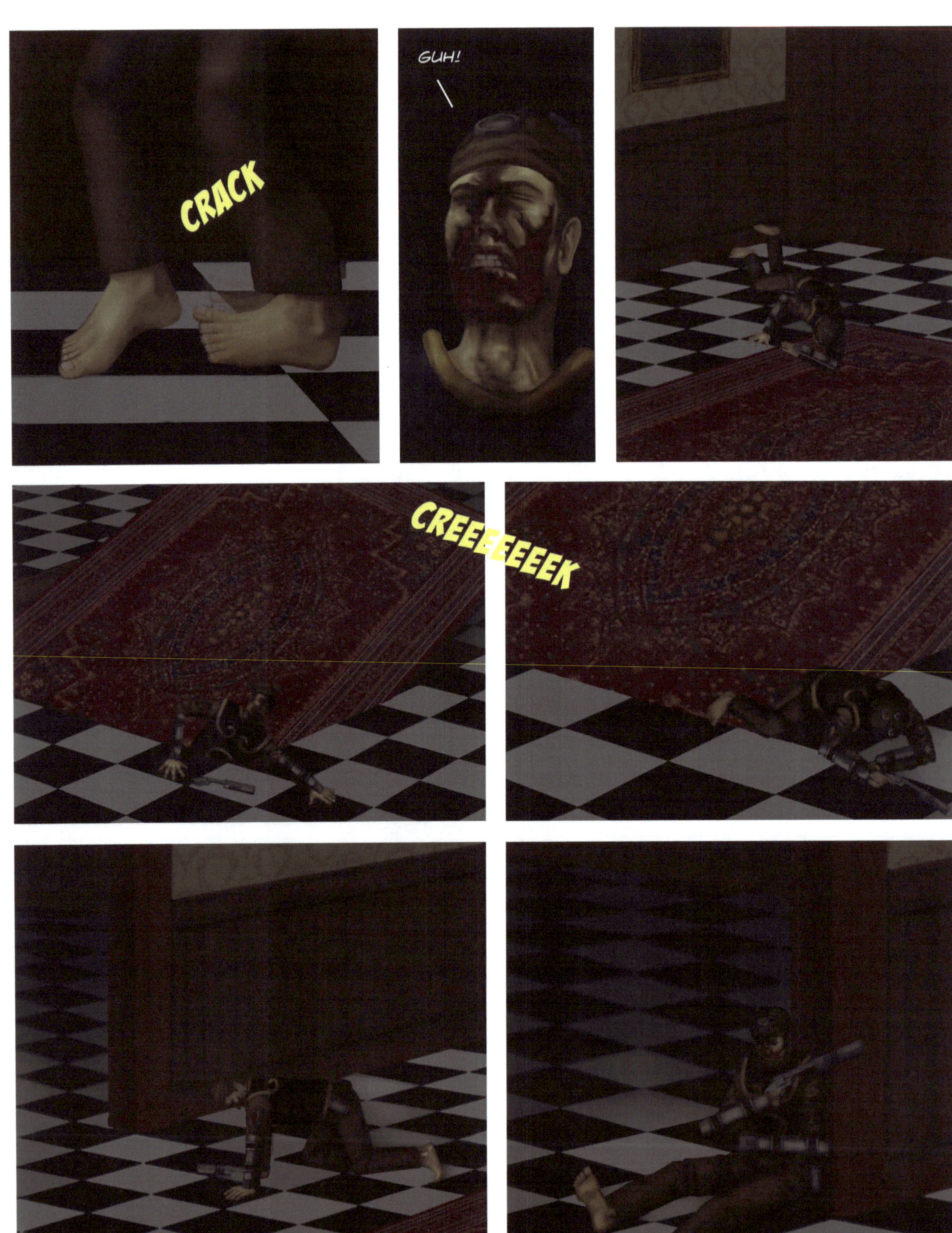

CRACK
GUH!
CREEEEEEK

I AM LOSING BLOOD.
AND MY FOOT IS BROKEN.

BUT IT'S TOO LATE TO QUIT.

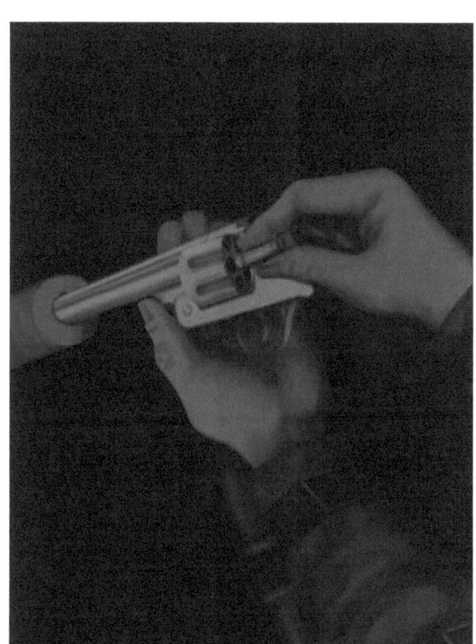

AUGUSTUS
LISTEN TO ME.

CONGRATULATIONS
I HAVE BEEN WOUNDED BY ONE OF YOUR SHOTS.
NOW THERE DOESN'T HAVE TO BE ANY MORE VIOLENCE.
JUST WALK AWAY AND I WILL NOT ALERT THE POLICE.
LET THIS BE OVER.

NOW YOU LISTEN TO ME!

YOU STOLE MY INVENTION!
YOU BURNED DOWN MY HOUSE!
AND YOU KILLED MY FAMILY!

I WILL WALK AWAY - - -

WHEN YOU ARE DEAD!

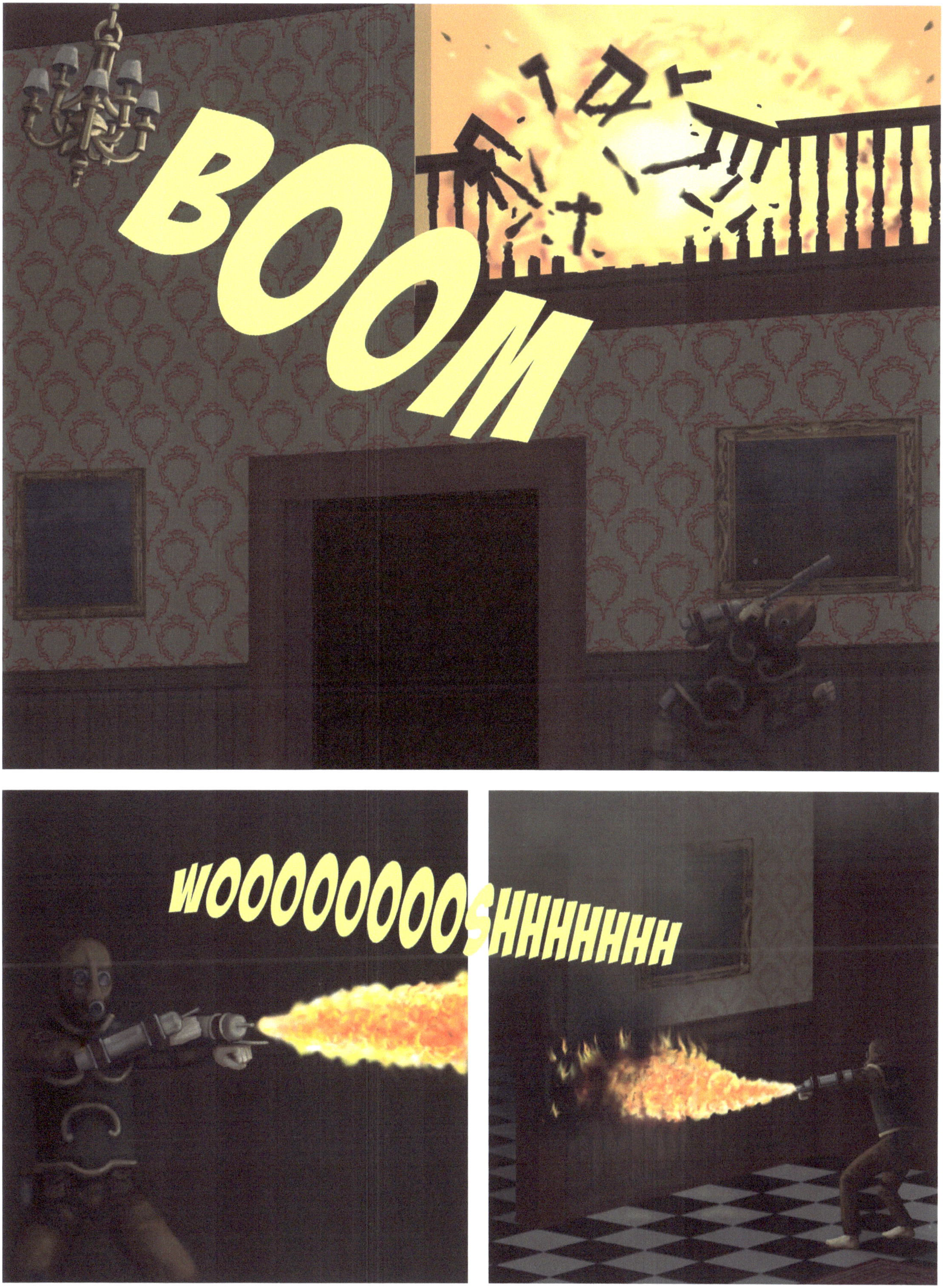

BOOM

WOOOOOOOOSHHHHHH

GAAAH!
I CAN'T WALK!

KOF
KOF

KOF
KOF

ANASTASIA . . .

DO NOT LEAVE ME.

PLEASE COME BACK.

NOOOOOOO!

GO AHEAD . . .
LET ME JOIN HER.

SHOOT
ME!
DO IT!
DO IT!

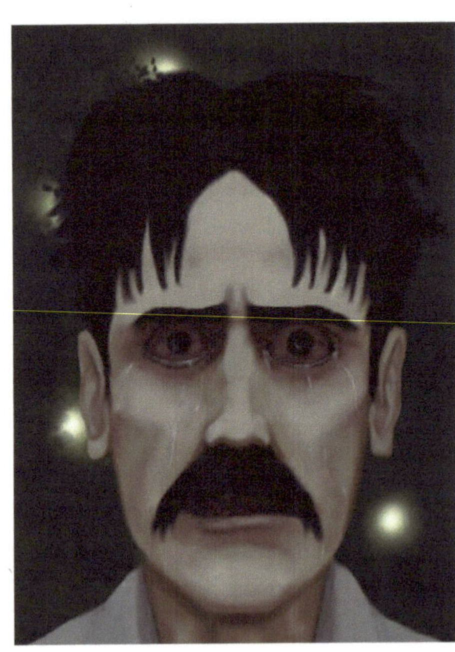

KRACK
KRACK
KRACK

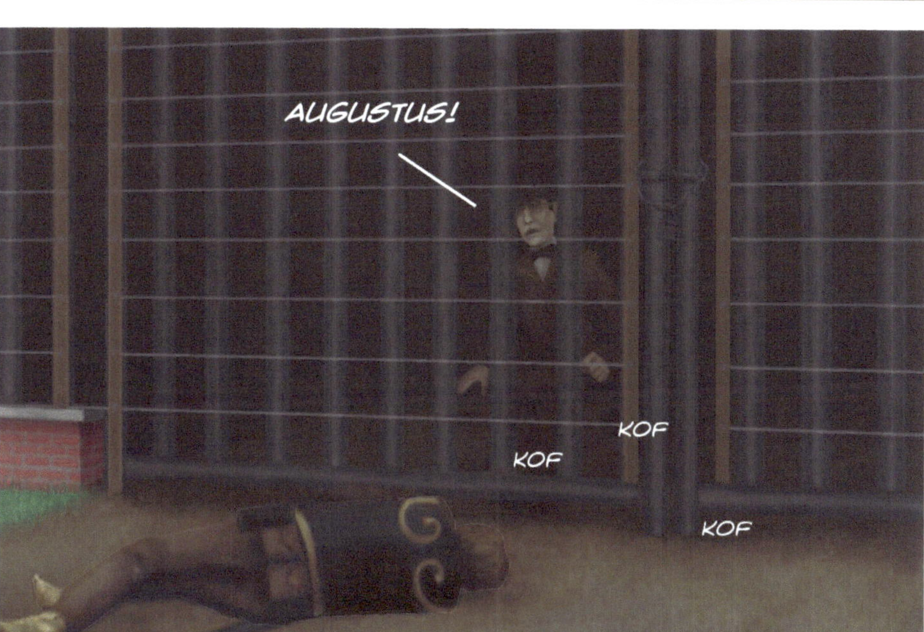

AUGUSTUS!
KOF
KOF
KOF

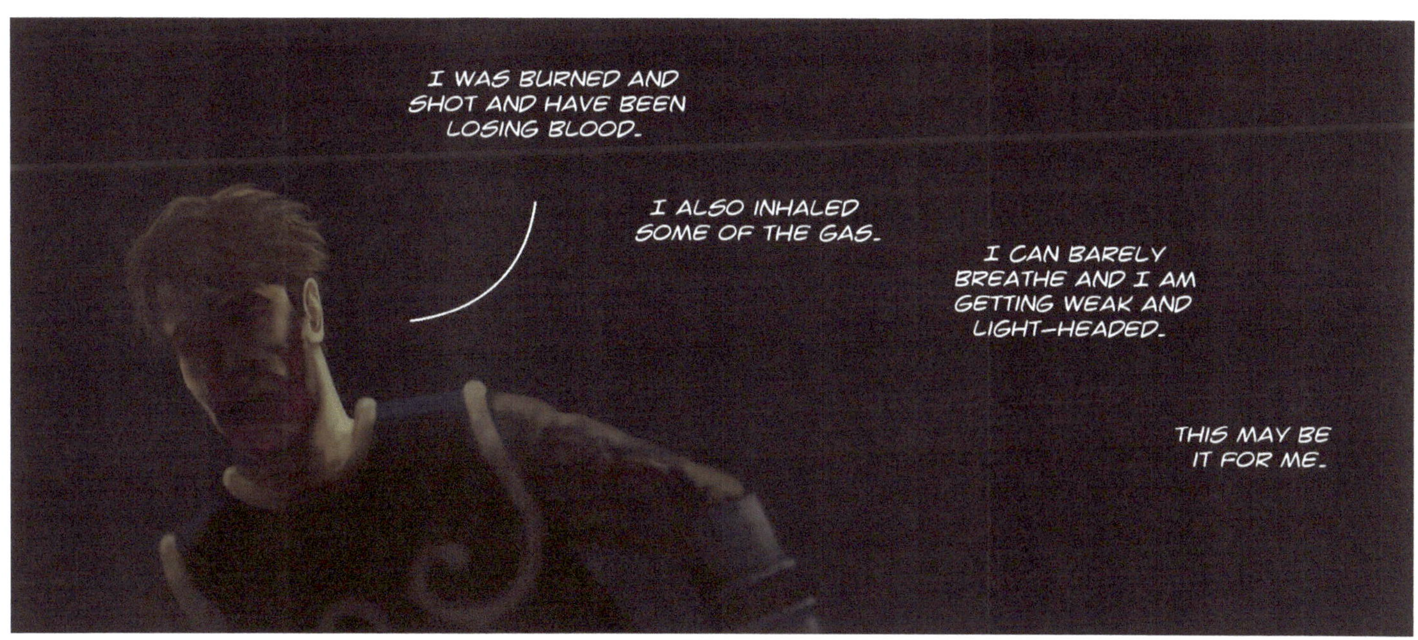

I WAS BURNED AND
SHOT AND HAVE BEEN
LOSING BLOOD.
I ALSO INHALED
SOME OF THE GAS.
I CAN BARELY
BREATHE AND I AM
GETTING WEAK AND
LIGHT-HEADED.
THIS MAY BE
IT FOR ME.

HAND ME THE KEYS AND I WILL GET YOU TO THE HOSPITAL.
IF I GO TO THE HOSPITAL I WILL BE ARRESTED.
AT LEAST HAND ME THE KEYS SO THAT I CAN GET YOU OUT OF HERE.
STAY WITH ME AUGUSTUS.
JUST HAND ME THE KEYS!
AUGUSTUS!
IT'S ALL RIGHT BENNY.
EVERYTHING IS ALL RIGHT.

AUGUSTUS . . .

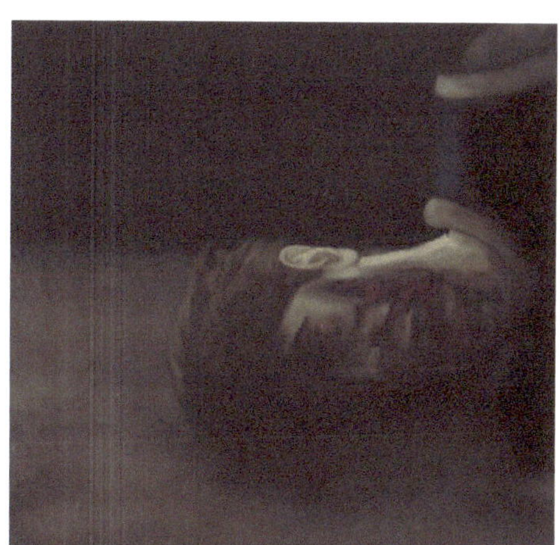

GOOD BYE
MY FRIEND.

The End

A NOTE FROM THE AUTHOR

Hello. This is Trenor. Thank you for reading my graphic novel. For those of you who might be interested I thought I should share a little behind-the-scenes history of this project.

Looking back everything happened so naturally that I cannot remember exactly how it started. I know that I was aware of a genre called "steam punk," as well as the rivalry that occurred between the inventors Edison and Tesla. I am assuming that I was subconsciously influenced by these things.

I initially wrote *The Lords of Invention* as a novella. It was a project that I worked on and off over the course of about three years. When it was finished I sent it out to literary agents, who showed no interest whatsoever in my little yarn. After coming to terms with that unfortunate fact, I shelved the manuscript and moved on to other things.

Years passed before I became aware of the works of the comic and graphic-novel writer Alan Moore. I was led into Moore's world through the film adaptation of his graphic novel: *V for Vendetta*. Moore's work showed me that comics could be more than super-hero stories. Inspired by what he was doing, as well as Frank Miller, creator of *300*, *Sin City*, etc., I embarked on the quest of turning my tale into a visual narrative.

I began this project by using more traditional ink line illustration; however, about a dozen pages in I realized that I was not satisfied with what I was seeing. Again, the project got shelved and more time passed.

It was not until I came across the graphic novel *Anomaly*, by Brian Haberlin, that the thought occurred to me that the entire story could be digitally painted. This appealed to me because I have always been more of a painter than a line artist. Although Haberlin had mostly used Photoshop to render his images, I was aware of a basic version of Photoshop called GIMP (GNU) that can be downloaded off of the internet for free—although donations are gladly accepted. Because of my previous failed attempts, I was able to get over my reluctance to spend hundreds of dollars on a program that might not even work out by using GIMP. I literally had nothing to lose. The more that I worked with GIMP the more that I liked it, and I ended up sticking with it even after I realized that I was going to commit to a fully digitally painted version of this work.

Although Haberlin had used 3D modeling software to initially render his characters, which he (or an assistant) then digitally painted over, I opted to go for a copy and paste approach. The copy and paste method is what made this work possible. Indeed, painting this in a more traditional method would have taken a life-time to complete. This method is similar to traditional animation techniques in which figures on a top layer are painted over a background on a bottom layer. Using this method allowed me to move characters and objects around on different layers without repainting every single panel over and over again.

Nevertheless, this copy and paste method did not prevent this project from being time consuming. It is difficult to say how much time that it took me because: (1) I never timed myself: (2) every page took a different amount of time to complete. I do know that I worked on it over a course of about four years, and the more that I worked on it the faster I got.

In regard to the story itself, I have been asked if I was influenced by the movie (or book) *The Prestige*, which also featured a tale of a rivalry between two men (albeit magicians) in the same approximate time period. Although I was aware of the movie,I doubt that it had any influence on me; especially due to the fact that when I eventually saw it I was disappointed with it (especially with how Tesla was portrayed). So I am leaning more towards The Prestige did not have any influence on me and that any similarities are only a coincidence. Also, in case any one was wondering if I got the idea for the title from the Frank Zappa's band *The Mothers of Invention*, the answer is: I am not sure. It's difficult to say what has influenced my subconscious over the years.

Anyway, thanks for checking out my book. I hope you enjoyed it.

- Trenor Rapkins

P.S. At the time of writing, Gimp does not have Smart Object and Adjustment Layer capabilities, nor the direct ability to convert RGB to CMYK color mode. Also, dealing with the pressure sensitivity function with drawing tablets can be a problem (The tips provided on the internet do not always work). For these reasons, I cannot recommend the use of Gimp for anything other than amateur projects. Although, these problems could be solved in future versions (I used 2.8).

A NOTE ABOUT THE BEAM GUN AND ITS HISTORY

Someone once told me that they liked my story except for the beam-gun part. According to this person, this particular contraption was too unbelievable. However, what this person and what you the reader may not know is that this weapon is based on an actual idea that was conceived by multiple inventors during that same time period, and is not outside the boundaries of scientific possibility. Indeed, particle beam weapons are currently being researched and developed in our own time as well. Examples of currently working directed energy beam weapons are lasers and microwave weapons.

I first became aware of this concept after watching a documentary on the life of Nikola Tesla. Tesla conceived of something that he referred to as a "death beam," or "teleforce" weapon. He was unable to construct a working model of his idea because he was unable to find a financial investor. It is most likely a good thing for humanity that this weapon was never created.

CONCEPT DESIGNS

The following pages are some of the original concept art/design that I constructed when I was working on the prose/novella version. As you may notice, many of these early ideas were later transferred over into the graphic-novel.

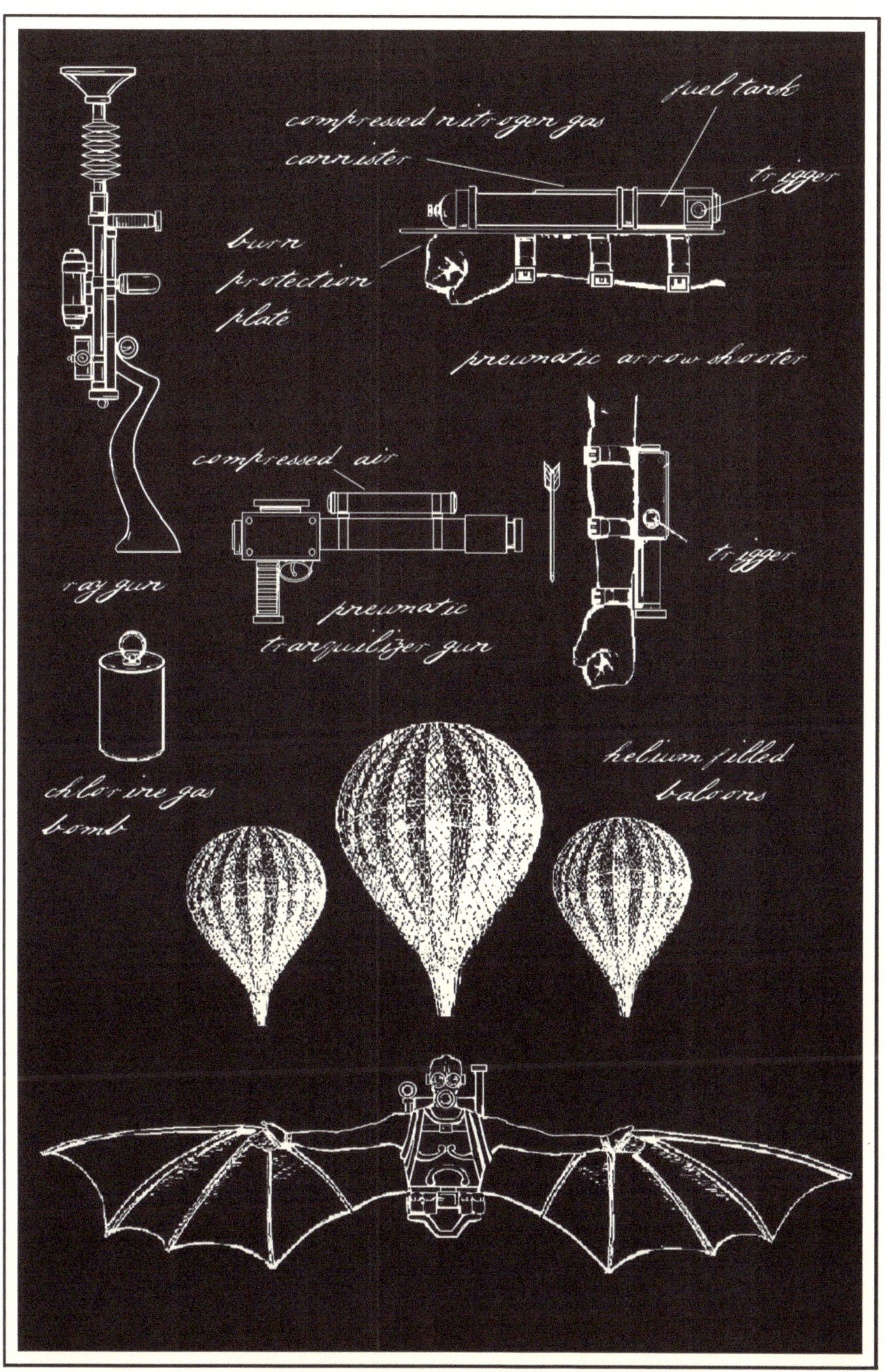

fuel tank
compressed nitrogen gas
cannister
trigger
burn
protection
plate
pneumatic arrow shooter
compressed air
ray gun
trigger
pneumatic
tranquilizer gun
chlorine gas
bomb
helium filled
baloons

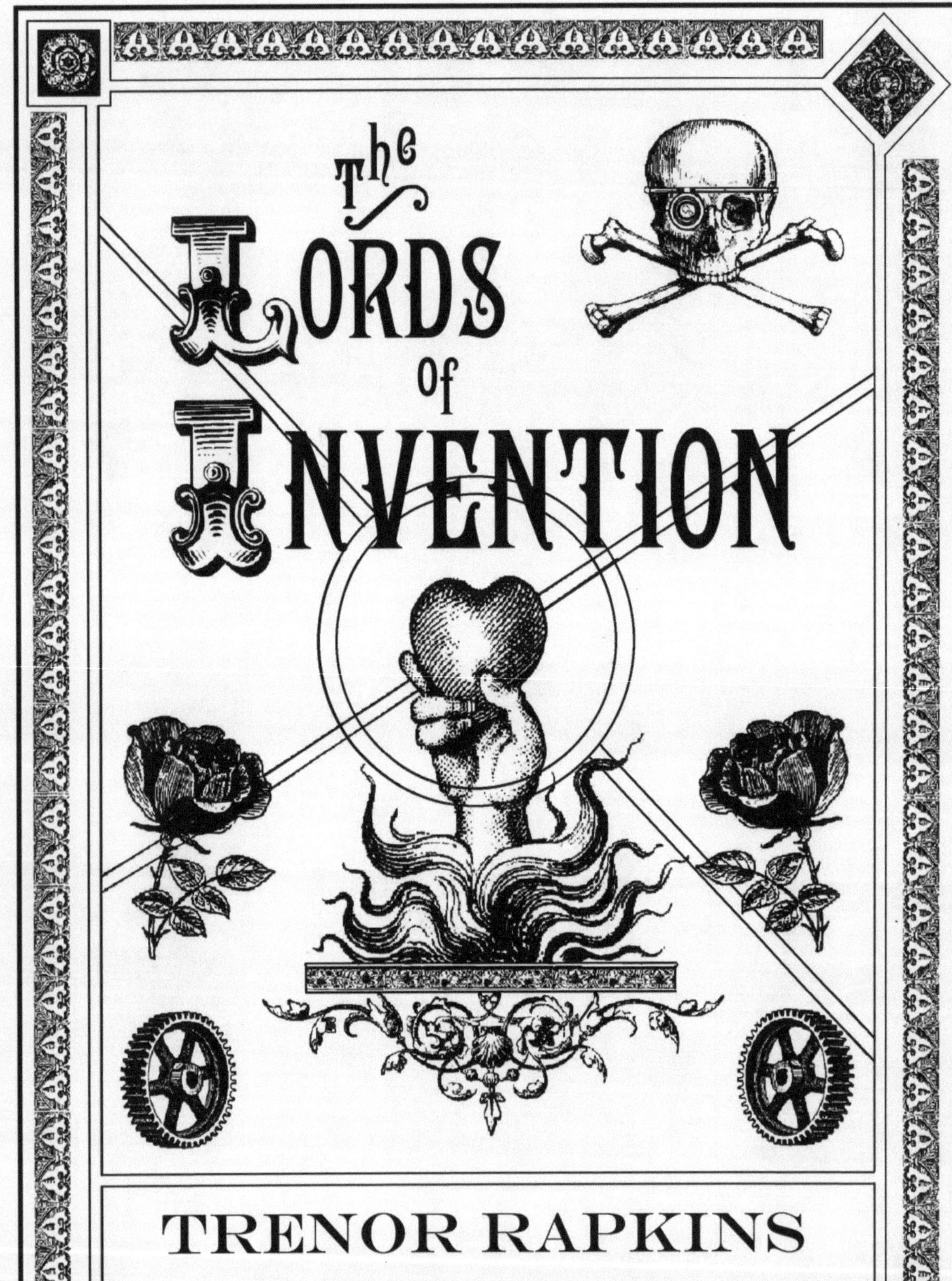
The
Lords
of
Invention

TRENOR RAPKINS